The Archivist
The Librarian Chronicles II

Published by
CHBB Publishing, LLC.

This is a work of fiction. All characters and events portrayed in this novel are fictitious and are products of the author's imagination and any resemblance to actual events, or locales or persons, living or dead are entirely coincidental.

Edited by Cheree Castellanos
Cover & Formatting by Pretty AF Designs

Letter from the author

Hi reader. Welcome to the second book in The Librarian Chronicles. I wanted to write a quick little letter first to thank those of you who helped make The Librarian such a successful story. In the author community it really does take a village. We do not have it easy, so when we find dedicated readers, we know how precious those people are.

This story is completely separate from The Librarian. You do not have to read book one to read book two. They are their own entities. While I do mention Emmeline in this book, you will not be confused by her entrance. There will be another book after this with a whole new story and new Librarian, so be prepared for more awesome time-traveling adventures.

Some things you should know about this book before diving in:

My teens are older teens, they are not children in high school and they sometimes curse and act like, well, normal young adults.

Before writing this book, I struggled with the language of which they would speak, because many people in the medieval Scottish era spoke Scottish Gaelic and Pictish. I wanted to convey that they do indeed speak their own language even though I wrote it in English and didn't put their dialect in the book. I struggled with how they would have conversations, because some Scot's do indeed talk with accents. Ultimately, I decided to forgo the normal accents in the dialogue, because it would become hard to follow for the reader.

This book was definitely hard to write. I didn't want it to be compared to Outlander at all, because it isn't anything like Outlander. Diana Gabaldon is a very talented author and her books are so amazing that many of them grace my shelves at home. When I began writing this story I wanted my character to go back in time to meet a real person from Scotland's history, but I didn't want the story to be scrutinized for taking on such a big task. So, I made my target, Sir Malcolm Walsh, similar to this Scottish hero. Let's see if you can see the similarities and figure out who I was referring to.

My character, Savannah, has had three names in this story. It took me that long to find a name I connected to! That has never happened before. But Savannah was chosen by my daughters and I just loved it.

With all that said, I hope you enjoy Savannah's story and her travels to Scotland.

Dedication

*For my grandpa Kennedy who gave me my Scottish heritage.
I honor you Grandpa and I miss your laugh.*

Prologue

"**S**avannah, as a librarian you** have been given a gift. One that not just anyone can handle. Most people wouldn't survive the trip across time," Mother explained as she played with my soft curls. I loved when she played with my hair. I was nestled up in my bed as she sat next to me. We were talking, again, about the gift of being part of the Bailey family. Our family was special, that I knew. I was a smart twelve year old and I knew how important this role was. The seriousness in Mother's tone was enough to drive that home. The many talks about my duty were coming more frequently the older I was getting.

"But when will I get to travel, Mother? I wish I could go now." I did wish that. Often. I wanted to be able to see the histories of our world just like she explained. I dreamt of traveling across time to distant lands, researching important men and women, who helped shape our world.

"I know darling, but you aren't old enough. I explained that. The job has to be passed on to you. And when Grandma passes away that will be your duty. I am trying to prepare you for your responsibilities. But school is also important. So focus on that for now, while you can."

I hated to think about life without Grandma in it. But I knew that would someday be a possibility. She was old and old people died. Like Grandpa did. I'll never forget his funeral and seeing his body in the casket. It was like looking at a plastic version of the man I used to know; it sort of looked like him but not quite. There were times I still couldn't believe he was gone. Poor Grandma was lost without him. But Mother said she had her work to keep her mind off of it. She traveled more often to keep herself busy, and I think staying away from the reminder of him was her goal.

Our family had a job to preserve the histories of the world. The Bailey family was vast. We stretched across America and some of us even lived in England according to Mother. She showed me on an old map that hung in Grandma's study. My grandma, my mom's mom, was part of a secret group of women called the Librarian's. They traveled through time to make sure that the history of certain influential people was correctly written. Once we traveled the books we would preserve that history, and the Librarian's job was done. Their purpose was to record the correct happenings in time, so that historians and writers didn't mess it all up. Grandma once told me that historians liked to stretch the truth about their research, and that our job was to make sure it was true. As we traveled, every detail was written in the blank pages of a book, so that nothing was kept out or lied about. Whether it was the writings of the traveler's guardian, or spontaneous writing while the Librarian traveled, it all became part of one big story. It still blew my mind at how it all worked. But then again, I had time to figure it out.

Grandma showed me once how they sealed the books and sent them to a larger historical library. I was antsy and wished I could be part of the family business sooner rather than later. I hated being a child.

"Savannah, I promise you, your time will come soon enough my impatient one. For now, just enjoy being a child while you can." She gave me the smile that made me feel like I was just that; a child. I hated how she called me impatient. And I despised how she babied me, so I rolled my eyes and rolled over. "Savannah, don't roll those eyes at me. I know you hate it but pretty soon you'll be part of it all. I wish I was, trust me. I won't be able to do what you do. The gift didn't pass on to me. You have no idea how much I wish it were mine"

There it was. The thing Mother always said to me. She wasn't given the gift of traveling so she always ended each talk with that last sentence. She closed the door gently and I knew I was alone. I turned on my headlamp and grabbed the book that Grandma had given me a year ago. It was what she called my *growing up gift*. The leather binding was soft and tan. The front cover was just as smooth as I ran my fingers over the title. Traveler's Guide. It was probably the most important thing anyone had ever given me. Even more so than the gold watch my dad gave me that used to be his father's. This guide was everything to a Librarian. That's what Grandma said.

Opening the front, I flipped to the title page. The duty of a Librarian was clearly typed and I loved the font so much, I read it over and over. It read: The Bailey women have always had gifts of old magic, and it is with that magic that they chose to protect history. The society of travelers maintain, protect, and preserve history, which make the world what it is today. As a story-preserver you may need to travel millions of years back in time. It is your duty to capture every moment accurately. You may never go forward in time, only back. Your duty requires you to always wear your tether, which is usually a piece of jewelry, and to never remove it while you're traveling. We're not to interfere with the inhabitants or their lives. As a Librarian you represent your family. Remember that this gift is yours and shouldn't be shared with anyone besides your protector.

I closed the book and my eyes with it. I fell asleep imagining where my first duty would take me.

One

Reaching up I effortlessly placed the book back in its spot. I looked down at my pile of books to be shelved and mentally counted how many stacks I would be visiting today. Thirteen shelves on the main floor and twelve on the upper level was all I had to shelve today. The upper level floor was my favorite. It housed the best fiction novels in our college library. The lower level was mainly school books, history, and nonfiction. Not that I minded being on this floor; I just preferred being up top. I'd gladly shelve all the books, no matter the type. There was something about being with them that made me feel at home. I loved my job here and I fought for it, too. As a freshman I must have been here every day begging the media specialist to hire me as an aid; not even an assistant. I just wanted to help, to just be around the books. She said no every time. Her excuses changed each day I visited. It wasn't until the middle of my summer vacation that she finally called on me. Her assistant had graduated and no one applied for the job. All the aids were happy being aids and I was the only one she met with such enthusiasm for the job. I had wanted it more than any of them anyhow. I knew it and so did they. Which is why I got the job. I was telling them what to do within two weeks of training. I was a fast learner and they hated me for it. I just ignored them and their petty jealousy. Being a book nerd is no easy task, but someone had to do it. So I stepped up to the plate.

"Hey Savannah!" I looked down, startled at first, and saw it was Trevor Arnold. The hottest and most popular guy on campus. He made the All Star team as a freshman, not that I cared about football one bit. But I did pay attention to Trevor. He was the guy of my dreams, and every other girl in this library from the looks of it. They either fanned themselves because of the heat of the North Carolina sun or from the hotness Trevor gave off as he walked by. It didn't matter what any girl was doing, they noticed Trevor. His body rivaled a god and his dark skin was like melted chocolate. He was beautiful. A dark-skinned man with light blue eyes and a fabulous personality that went along with it. Trevor really cared about people. He never hated on or was mean to anyone. His friendliness was addicting and it rubbed off on me. I'll admit when I first started my freshman year I was in my Emo-phase. I was angry at the world and always so emotionally distant with everyone on campus. Then I met Trevor. He was one of my first friends here, just when I needed one, too, because I was feeling more alone than ever before. My mom was two hours away and I didn't have a car to visit her or anyone from back home. My roommate was always out partying and that wasn't my thing; not that I didn't try. But remember the Emo-phase I mentioned? I didn't do parties then, I read books and stayed inside.

Now, maybe I'd do one or two but school is important to me and so was this job.

"So, are you and I going to talk about this?" Trevor held up a paper that was marked with a huge A in red ink.

"What is there to talk about? You asked me and I did it. It's not a big deal, Trev. So don't make it one. Okay?" I rolled my eyes and began the climb down from the ladder. I didn't feel totally comfortable talking about this with him, but I didn't regret doing it, because he was my friend. He was struggling and if he didn't pass that exam, he would fail Lit. I couldn't do that to him. I had the brains and I'd practically written that paper in my sleep. What's done was done.

"Savannah, you aren't my friend so that you can write my Lit papers. You're my friend because I like your company." He flashed those pearly whites and I stopped climbing. I wondered all the time why I wasn't more than a friend. Didn't he notice that I liked him? He had to.

"Just say, 'thank you, Savannah' and go back to class."

He softly rested his hand on my shoulder and said, "Thank you. You're a lifesaver." After a quick hug he was gone. As I watched him walk away a feeling struck me inside. It was one I tried to ignore millions of times, but it kept coming back. No. Trevor wasn't using me. He wouldn't do that. He's a good guy. A great friend who just needed some help with his Lit paper. That's all. It's a one-time thing and I'd never do it again.

"You know he's using you, right?"

God. I just wanted to shelve books and then ... well I had things to do after everyone left. Jessa Walsh insisted on being that little annoying angel on my shoulder. If Trevor Arnold was the most popular guy on our campus, then that made Jessa the belle of all of North Carolina. She was the epitome of southern charm. Her adorable face and rocking body made all the guys fall at her heels. And she was my friend. I liked to look at her as my friend that I never asked for. She just came with the job. Jessa was the only one who worked with me that didn't hate me for my position. You could say we were thrown together; literally.

"Shut your hole, Jessa," I said, passing by her with my cart. "You're just jealous that Trevor doesn't want to be around you anymore."

She laughed, and it sounded like little ringing bells. "His loss, Savannah. You know that he could have had me, but instead he went for Lacey Halston, and then Ariana Black, and then—"

"Okay! I get it. He likes girls. All girls but me. Let's not throw it in my face, okay?"

She followed me to the elevator and squeezed in between me and the huge cart. She was wearing a dainty little dress with Keds and she pulled it off so well. Me, I was not a dress girl. I tried very hard not to wear them. Not even to weddings or fancy outings. Jessa once asked me to a ball that her family hosted and I wore pants. I don't care. I am who I am. My body wasn't small or petite by any means. I am curvy and fluffy, as I like to refer to it. Other people call me husky or chunky. That's okay. I used to be heavier than I currently am and they didn't know that I lost fifty pounds my senior year of high school by going vegetarian, and that's fine. I looked at myself as real. Jessa dieted constantly and her body didn't change. When I dieted I lost a whole toddler. So now I maintain and try to help Jessa feel better about what she looks like; which is so royally fucked up. You know that there is something wrong with our world when the skinny girl has an eating disorder and the curvy girl goes to town on a veggie burger and fries.

"Savannah, girl, you are beautiful. You're too good for him. He's using you for your brain and you let him. I don't understand it, but it's your life." She threw her hands up in her cute little way. I loved when Jessa got frustrated.

"Yes, Jessa. This I know. It's my life. What are you doing here anyway? You're not due in for two more hours?" I asked as I looked at my phone.

Only Jessa would come to work early. "We're still doing it tonight?"

I nodded and the doors opened exposing the second floor. "Yes, just go home. You don't need to be here."

She hugged me and I left the elevator. "I don't know how you stay so calm about it all. I feel antsy. Maybe I'll go to the gym to calm myself."

I snickered. "Yeah I'm the one who does all the work and you're antsy. Weirdo. Yes, go be calm at the gym. Goodbye, Jessa."

I pressed the button and the doors closed. Jessa was like a hamster, always moving. I sighed and rolled my cart to my favorite stack; fantasy.

Was I nervous about tonight? Yes. I always was. But it was my duty and I had to do it. No one else here understood that besides Jessa. They all thought that I was nerdy Savannah Preston. Underneath this lovely exterior was a girl who could literally change the world. I wasn't just working at the library because I loved books. No, it was more than that. This library housed something very precious to my family. Two years ago my grandma sat me down and talked to me seriously about my future. I had been waiting for that moment since I was twelve. She told me that I was more than just a Preston. I was also a Bailey and I held a gift to travel through time. When she died last year, I had been given a job that involved more than just going to college. I was now the new traveler and my duty was mine to have. I looked down at the bracelet that once graced her arm. It held a special jewel that held the power to tether me to this time, no matter where I was in the past, this bracelet kept my physical body here while my spiritual or mental body was in another place in time. To say it was precious was an understatement. If I were to lose it, I wouldn't be able to safely travel back to my own time and my physical body would be pulled back in time. I'd be risking being stuck and that I couldn't do. It could alter the future by doing so.

I began shelving the fantasy books, many of which were checked out to me, and I tried not to worry about my task tonight. Even though Jessa saw a calm woman standing before her didn't mean I didn't get nervous about traveling through time. I just hid it way better than she did. I took a deep breath in then let all the air out of me. With it went the stress that followed me around all day like a ghost.

****

"I got us smoothies with kale!" There was something so wrong with smoothies made with vegetables. Jessa knew I didn't like those two things in combination, but she always bought them for me. She held up the green cups of goo and followed me down the stairs. We had been meeting in the library basement after every shift we worked. The only times we didn't meet was when we had class or days off. This way we knew the basement was clear of prying eyes. Jessa had just finished her shift and let me in after she locked the doors. We both made sure that the whole library was clear and we headed down stairs. I found this little section in the basement when I was looking through a box of books for the media specialist, Ginger. It was the perfect space for Jessa and I to work and we claimed it as ours six months ago.

The basement was as big as the library but held lots of doors and storage spaces. This room was completely empty. I had to move a shelf aside to get to the door that led to the room, but it was worth every bruise I received. Jessa had brought pillows and strung up lights to help us relax. I didn't tell her that it didn't help me in any way, but she wouldn't care. She liked the mood it set and I just let it go. What Jessa found relaxing helped me because it kept her quiet. And a quiet Jessa was a good Jessa.

While there were no windows in the room, it didn't bother us. We did find pictures to adorn the walls and that seemed to make it less like a prison. I sat at the desk and Jessa plopped down on the bean bag that she bought last week.

"Are you ready to go yet or do you want to go over what we learned last week?" she asked, thumbing through the notebook she held.

I sipped the goo and bit back my gag.

"I think I'm fine," I said, trying not to throw up. "I just need to find out where he went between 1298 and 1304. I can handle that." I smiled and Jessa laughed so hard she almost spit out her smoothie.

"You have kale in your teeth! You can't go into the book like that! Can you imagine?" She laughed and I couldn't help but laugh along with her. I liked grossing

Jessa out. What she found gross I saw as normal. She wouldn't dare go outside with a fresh face. God forbid people see Jessa without makeup on. She was a true princess through and through. She even had the tiaras from winning pageants. I blamed her parents for making her the way she was. She had absolutely no confidence in herself, even though she was essentially perfect. Her blonde long hair was always glossy, but that didn't stop her mom from saying things like; *"You need a haircut, your ends are fried"* Or my absolute favorite, *"Oh Jessa, stop trying to embarrass me and fix your face."* Her father never said things like that but he allowed his wife to say hurtful things, and that was just as bad in my eyes.

When I first met Jessa at my grandma's funeral I hated her. Upon first impression, I walked away thinking she was pretentious and rude. She wore a pink dress to a funeral. I mean, who does that?

Then when I found out she was going to be my protector, I hated her even more. Jessa's parents were high society and they were involved with my family in dealings with historical artifacts. They didn't know my ancestors traveled through time, but they knew we were important historians and that we preserved facts. My grandma thought Jessa would be a good match to help me. I thought that she was senile and wrong and that it wasn't going to work out, but I was wrong. We learned to like each other and then we became best friends. Turns out my grandma *was* right.

Jessa was my guide and I need more than just her friendship. While I travel through time she watches over me, keeping me safe. Jessa is also responsible for making sure my clothing is appropriate for the time frame, while also assisting me while I chronicle what I have seen and what experiences I've gone through. She keeps notes on all of these things in her guide book, which basically makes her invaluable to me and to the work that I do. In order to travel through time, you must have a guide you can trust, and I trust Jessa with my life.

The most important research was kept inside the blank pages of a book. Each mission yielded a new book. Once that book was full and our mission complete, it was sealed. I'm a Librarian, but not in the typical sense. I haven't earned the proper diploma to get such a title. I, along with many others throughout the world, preserve the history of some of the most famous historical figures inside the blank pages of each book we are sent. The Librarians was founded by a famous scientist, Harold Lockhart. Lockhart wrote the formula for time travel in the only thing he had near him when it was fresh in his brain. That book wasn't empty, it happened to be the history of none other than, Abraham Lincoln. After he wrote the formula, he was whisked away in time and came face to face with Lincoln himself. The talent to travel and record history was never his intention, but after he realized how wrong historians were about the president, he created the group of Librarians. Lockhart put us in charge of libraries and their books. The sect of Librarians were given their jobs and they went to work straight away.

I myself hope to achieve the goal of working in a library with the official title someday, which is what I'm studying in school. My intention is to host my own library and help archive important time periods through my research as well as artifacts, like my grandma did.

Like all the women did who came before her.

All I know about my job before I travel is who I'm to research. Everything else is learned while I'm *inside* the book, or in other words, the past.

I'm forbidden to change history by becoming involved in the past or with my target. But I can become friendly with them and immerse myself in their world. It's hard not to become part of it. While I'm there I am more than just a girl recording the true history. I become my character fully and truly; as if I really am who I say I am. I've been many different people, traveling five separate times into five people's lives. And each time I go, I'm nervous. It doesn't take long to fill the pages the Historical Society of Libraries sends me. I'm currently one of the youngest on the East Coast. My job is taken extremely seriously, for I have wanted to do this for a long time. Now that it's my job, I feel as if I am living the dream.

How could I not love it? I am a college student full time and on my off days I travel to the past. What is there not to like?

Jessa would argue that I don't have a social life, which is true, but I don't care. I'm social in the past, so that should count for something. I talk to people on campus but I don't need friends right now, I need to do this job and make my family and late grandma proud.

"So, did you bring the looser fitting dress this time?" I asked Jessa as I pulled the book from a safe hiding place. She held up a dress with a blue fabric that probably would fit better than the size she made prior. Jessa is handy with costumes. She makes all my clothing and tells her parents it's for school plays. Which is why we donate them afterward to the drama club. They're always thankful and it shows up on stage somehow.

"I took out the waist a bit. Should fit much better this time around." She handed me the dress and I thoroughly inspected the fabric. It's perfect. "I had to visit three different fabric shops to find this, you know?"

"How could I forget? You've told me now, let's see, that makes five times! Jessa, thank you so much. Did I mention how *thankful* I am?" I rolled my eyes dramatically but really, I was thankful. Everything Jessa does is perfection and I realized every time how right my grandma was about her. As I got dressed Jessa readied my spot so that I could sit comfortably. She spoils me but then she does stuff like buy me kale smoothies. I laughed to myself about how awful it tasted but then realized that she thinks this is what delicious is. She's so wrong, I feel as if it is my job, as her friend, to show her how wrong she is. Grabbing my stash of chocolate, I dropped it in her lap.

"No! I will not eat that while you're inside. No way. I have a date this weekend and my parents would kill me." She said all this while eyeing the dark chocolate candy bar and I know I've set the trap. That kale crap will be in the trash when I get back. Pulling my dark auburn hair back and braiding it into a renaissance fashion prepares me for the actual look of the time period. Once finished, I looked in the mirror and removed all of my kohl liner and lipstick. I only go inside with a bit of rouge on my cheeks and lips. I have to look the part completely.

"How do I look?" Wearing a dress is the epitome of awful for me but Jessa's eyes lit up.

She clapped her hands and said, "Beautiful and very peasant like." Frowning, I looked down at the blue tartan gown Jessa made me and realized, I did look like a peasant, but that's all right. I'm not trying to be noticed; the goal is to blend in. I've learned Gaelic and Celtic in many different forms, which prepared me for my first visit to medieval Scotland. Their dialect was strange at first but it soon became second nature. I hear them and understand them as clearly as I hear my peers and more importantly, I seem like I belong while I am there. Even though I am only a visitor, I feel immersed in Scotland.

My target, Sir Malcolm Walsh, is not a well-known man in today's society, but in the fourteenth century, he was a big deal. He fought battles and saved many villages from torment of the English King. My research is to know more about him and where he went for the six years he seemed to drop off the face of the earth, until his capture and death in 1304. I've already met him and become involved with his friends. And by involved I mean, I know their faces and they know I am the scullery maid who pops in occasionally. When I enter back in, they don't question a thing. I can be gone for as long as a week or a month, but I always arrive where I'm needed. The book knows what I need and will deliver me to my destination. The men and Sir Malcolm are always brutes and can sometimes be callous, but never with me. I think that they see me as a naïve girl who is extremely homely looking. While she readied the hem of my dress, I took off my glasses and put in contacts. It's important that I do not lose them while there. I could see a little bit, but it would be hard.

"Do you think I look bad?" I asked as Jessa started to inspect the dark chocolate further. She finally graced me with her gaze and said, "No, not bad, but perfect for the, you know, time period. I think that if you were to wear the other dress I made, you would look even better. You should also let your hair down." She got up and fumbled with my braid until my hair fell across my shoulders. After a few minutes and a tug of my dress to expose my bosom, she handed me the mirror. She's right! She let my hair down but braided a crown atop my head and added some flowers which were indeed real. My chest was pushed up to the maximum height, because that's how they did it back then, but I felt all kinds of uncomfortable.

"Now you look sexy and less peasanty. Gotta show off those tatas girl!"

I rolled my eyes. "I absolutely loathe it when you call them that."

"Which is *why* I say it. Now," she said as she handed me the book. "Get going before we run out of time." She kissed my cheek and I sat down in my spot. Every time I go in, I'm nervous but for some reason, I wasn't this time. I opened the book to the marked page and pulled out the red ribbon book marker. And before I knew it, I felt a rush and was standing in the middle of a battlefield.

Two

I've been dropped into some strange places while researching Sir Malcolm, but this really takes the cake. I was surrounded by thousands of dead bodies and maybe some still living. I tried hard not to look at them, but it's difficult not to want to go to them and help them. While I'm in this world I cannot prevent natural occurrences from taking place or altering the future of anyone. Doing so could mean altering the past.

The amount of blood that laid across this field was stifling and the stench made it difficult to breathe. I actually felt like puking or perhaps passing out, but I didn't want to fall on the dead man that lay near me. It was then that I heard something behind me. I wasn't sure if it was good or bad, or if I could end up laying here bloody and dead with the rest of these Scots, but before I could even determine it, I was scooped up and taken by the waist. The rider atop the horse had me in his clutches and I didn't wail or cry, I just held on and prayed he wasn't an Englishmen bent on hurting me or killing me. Or worse.

Once we crossed the field he gently let me down.

"Are you okay, lassie?" I silently thanked God and sighed. Answering him in his native tongue I said, "I am. Thank you for helping me. What happened out there?"

Shaking his head he hopped down from his horse and replied, "Nasty fight that was. We were all lucky to get out of it before we ended up like those poor bastards. God rest their souls." He looked me over and then down at the bottom of my dress. "Aye lass, you're clean as a daisy in spring. How did that come about?"

Thankfully I've learned to be quick with my responses, which basically meant I lied really well. "Fell off my horse, I did. Stupid ox got spooked and thankfully I landed on my feet or I would have ruined my garment."

"Aye, you're indeed lucky. I haven't seen your horse, but we might find him if we ride up to the hillside a bit more. This is no place for you, I assure you."

I bashfully smiled and nodded my head. "Where does the hillside lead? I'm afraid I'm lost. I'm supposed to be with Sir Malcolm. I work for him, in the kitchens, and was out for a ride when I got turned around."

It's then that I became caught in my lie, because he delivered a look of mass confusion. "Must have been a long ride, lass. Sir Malcolm has been away for months. What did you say your name was?"

I never used my real name. Unfortunately for me, Savannah isn't often used in this time period. In fact, it's never used in any time period I have visited.

I actually hated my name and never thought it fit me as a person. It's more the name of a southern belle like Jessa.

When I started traveling I decided to reinvent myself and gave myself the name Mollie. It's Welsh in origin but still means the same as the name intends in Scottish Gaelic.

So no one ever doubted it and I never stood out. Having an alias was helpful in any time period, I found, but mostly in this one. Having a name that made you stand out was not what I wanted for my trips.

"Pleased to meet your acquaintance. My name is Mollie. I've been Sir Malcolm's maid for over a year," I tell him truthfully. I have been traveling with him through several of his years, but only a few short months of my time. "I went out to retrieve a list of items needed in the kitchens from Iona, she is still the cook isn't she?" He nodded but said nothing. "I've been deterred, that is true. I fell ill during my ride. A lovely lass in town helped me heal. It's been a long arduous ordeal and I'd like to just go home, if that's all right with you. Now what did you say your name was?"

He harrumphed as he now realized that my story may have panned out and he didn't have the advantage any longer. The men in this time period were so rough around the edges and downright rude to women, and the small feminist side of me wanted to punch him in the nose. I hated how awful they were at times but considered myself very lucky to be in the care of Sir Malcolm and his men. They always made sure no one messed with the women of their houses.

"I didn't say my name, but I will now," he said, full of piss and vinegar, all of a sudden. "Finn O'leary, is my name. And I'll be taking you to our camp now. So if you don't mind, lass, I'd like to leave the dead to their dying."

I obliged and hopped onto his horse. While he walked, I rode. The view was spectacular and I realized that I missed the Scottish lands so much that I almost began to weep openly. I pulled it together though, because Finn would probably find it odd that I'm crying, but then again us women are nuts, so it might not be too weird. The weather had a chill that began to take hold as we entered the hillside. A low lying fog that appeared out of nowhere began to sweep across the grass and move swiftly over Finn's feet. Scotland is strange like that. You can be enjoying a sunny day and all of a sudden it downpours on you. I don't question it until Finn started rushing the horse faster up the hill and away from the fog.

"Everything okay down there, Finn?" I asked.

"Mind if I get on with you? I think I can get Frith to go faster that way."

He's scared. Of what, I didn't know but I don't ask a thing. Instead, I moved back on Frith, which also means deer forest, and let Finn onto his horse. He kicked the horse and without warning we were hauling up the hillside faster than I expected. Frith is fast for a fat horse who is in desperate need of exercise. They probably don't take care of their animals at this camp and I wouldn't be surprised if they rode them until they died and then moved on to another horse.

The horsemaster should be ashamed. I love horses and to see this animal run like hell out of these woods, makes me worried for it. And a bit for myself too, because why *is* he running like this.

"What's out there?" I dared to ask.

Finn shook his head and did that grumpy noise in his throat like he did before. "Can't say. But you should keep quiet, if you value your life."

He didn't have to tell me twice before I shut my mouth and stayed silent. As we crested the top of the hill and cleared the trees in the thick forest, the fog went away and Frith slowed down. Finn patted him and promised loads of oats and water upon our arrival. Arrival to where I wasn't sure because there was absolutely nothing out here.

The trees that were so green below were starting to turn orange up here. Another odd thing about this place; two different seasons at once. It's fall which meant I've been gone for three months, at least. I had really hoped I would catch Sir Malcolm before he left to wherever he was going. The whole point was to find out where he was hiding. I can't give up. There is still a chance someone at his camp will give me the location and I can find him easily enough. I couldn't help but miss Jessa, even though I've only been here for an hour or so. I had just wondered if she ate the candy when I saw it.

It was like something out of a fairytale. A long winding path, made from trees that have been bent over to form an archway that spans the length of the road in front of us. Frith took us into it and we were enveloped in leafy darkness. The sun just barely poked enough light for the horse to see. I reached up and touched it and the leaves tickled my palms as I passed underneath. Where this leads, I don't know, but I could stay here all day long. It was unlike anything I'd seen before.

"We're here, lass. Get your hands down." I looked up and that's when I saw what he meant and pulled my hands back sharply. The ending of the archway was full of thorns and sharp wooden stakes that would have gashed my hands open like a knife through butter.

"Thanks for the warning, Finn," I said. "Where is this path leading us? Or can I no longer speak?"

"You're a feisty one aren't you? No wonder you're a maid. Probably can't shut your crabbit mouth for two seconds."

He probably thought insulting me would make me angry, but instead I laughed out loud and said, "I could keep myself quiet. I just need to be asked nicely, that's all. And I am not bad tempered, I'm actually very pleasant."

"I don't plan to get to know the *help*. I have work to do. Go make yourself useful in the kitchens. I'm sure Iona would be happy to see you're alive and well," he said as he yanked the horse to a stop. "You can walk the rest of the way."

What a jerk! I didn't say a word in reply. I did as he said and got down from Frith, but not before thanking him for riding so fast. I turned from Finn O'Leary, and his nasty demeanor, and walked away like the respectful young lady I am. I looked away from him and into the unknown up ahead of me. The thorn bushes led the rest of the way in, but Frith carried his master away from me, probably to the stables. I had half a mind to follow just to see who exactly cared for the horses, but I had to get to Iona first. Establishing my residence here is priority number one.

I didn't expect the walk to take so long and my feet began to kill me after only a few minutes. The shoes were horrible and despite the cold air around me I started to feel hot and sweaty in this dress. Being sweaty in the cold is a dangerous thing, so I sped up my walking despite the pain it caused me.

Before I knew it I reached the end and saw the second most amazing site since my arrival. The castle before me is no camp, it's absolutely beautiful. I realized we're so far up the mountain that the air is thinner and colder, but it makes sense. If I were hiding from my English enemy, this would be where I'd hide. Far away from where prying eyes would see me. I too would take my people somewhere safe, even if the landscape wasn't safe. The castle in front of me was made of stone and looked like it could withstand a fight, but what did I know about architecture? My job here is to see if historians got it right or not. They make mistakes all the time and they actually have no solid proof of Sir Malcolm's hideaway.

I was in no rush to get back home to North Carolina. Scotland is the most beautiful place I'd ever visited. Each time I come, I feel as if I am home.

I always referred to myself as a *lost girl*. I never belonged in my life. I always felt as if I was an old soul, compared to my friends and peers. I never liked the same things they did, and never did follow the fads that my generation acquired. I always stood back from the crowds and kept away from those people who made it their life's purpose to take so many selfies that they all just began to look the same. Another thing I veered away from was the language of my so-called equals. You'd never catch me saying words like; bae, totes, or fleek. I was old school. I use proper English and respect my elders. And yes, books are my passion and I also like gardening. My grandma thought that I was born too late. She always said, "God just forgot to release you into the world is all. He kept you with him just a little longer." She also said that one day I would fit in; but I thought otherwise. I surrounded myself with books and Jessa and that was it. With the exception of Trevor, I never really liked guys my age. They were always so immature. I was glad to have at least one guy I could find attractive at my university.

I never fit in with my family either. With my mother, and her mission to turn me into a proper young lady of the south, and my mission to do nothing of the sort, our relationship was strained from then on. We rarely spoke. Not that I had ill will toward her, but after our last argument,

I chose to not call her. My father left us when he found a better *calling*, as he called it. Moving to Japan to be with his girlfriend he met there on business was his calling. His new children are his life now and I am but an afterthought. My mother fell apart after he left. I was thirteen and all I had was my grandma. She told me that life was full of uncertainties and marriage was one of them. I gave my mother time to grieve but she still hasn't gotten it out of her system yet. She found focusing on me and getting me perfect, and to her liking, to be her distraction from the pain. For a while I went along with it, but after seventeen, I threw in the towel. I wouldn't go to another debutante ball again. Now our arguments are different, but we still don't talk much.

Being lost doesn't mean that I *will* ever be found. It isn't lost on me that part of the reason I love to time travel is to hopefully find where I belong. As I walked into the castle entrance, I knew it wasn't here. Medieval Scotland isn't the time period I am meant for. Call me a prude, but I just can't get over the lack of indoor plumbing and bathing in the spring only. The castle was busy with people scurrying this way and that and it wasn't too hard to track down someone to lead me into the kitchens. I could hear the women chattering away as no doubt they were roasting some huge pig. It was Iona's specialty. I walked into the room and caught the eye of the beautiful cook whom I made such good friends with.

Three

"Oh my word! Mollie, you've come back to us!" Iona shouted from clear across the kitchen. The smell of roast pig hit my nose and my mouth watered instantly. Iona's black curls had begun to come undone underneath her cap and she quickly tucked them in before hugging me tightly. "We thought you for dead, lass. Where have you been?"

I began to tell her my fake story about catching ill as she readied me a plate with fresh bread and cheese. She laid it in front of me and I foolishly looked around for a knife before I remembered there are no utensils in this time. I picked up the bread and ate slowly, still telling her my tale. Iona bought it apparently because she hugged me closer saying a quiet prayer thanking God for my safe homecoming.

"I was hoping to find work here once more," I said, taking a break between bites. "Is my job still mine, then?"

Her smile lit up her face as she said, "Your duty as scullery maid is no more. Gwen has taken that job in your absence. But I do need another pantry keeper to help me keep the pantry stocked. I also need you to help me serve the feast that's about to begin. So go see Marsen and get some proper kitchen attire on before those buffoons start staring at those." She pointed to my chest. I turned red all over and the blush didn't go away even as Marsen dressed me in the same dress and cap as Iona. I felt bland and perfectly content in these clothes but awful that when I got back home, Jessa's dress would be lost forever.

My time here always varied. I never knew when I would disappear from this time and go back home. When I did, I literally disappeared as if I was taken away by magic. Well, science can be a sort of magic, I suppose. I knew when my time was almost up when I began to feel a tugging at my soul. Jessa said that sounded weird but there was no other way to describe the feeling. She also said that my eyes would flutter crazily as my physical body lay in front of her. She knew that it was almost time for me to come back, so she would sing to me. I could always hear her singing so I knew it was time. I found a spot out of the way, hidden from sight, to travel away from this time. I hated scaring people or causing alarm. The last thing I needed was to be accused of witchcraft upon my return and hanged or even worse, burnt alive.

The first time I traveled, Jessa freaked out that my physical body stayed behind and not my whole self. I always found it hard to believe myself that we each had a spirit. This spirit side was what traveled through the book. Unless I took off my bracelet. Doing that took your physical body into time wholly, which made things much more dangerous. You could get lost forever in time.

I always kept it hidden well and never let anyone see it. It wasn't easy to hide when you worked in the kitchens, like I was currently doing. In times like this, I slid it as far up my arm as it would go. I hurriedly prepared the large platter of some sort of meat Iona made and handed it to a young girl whose name I had yet to learn. I grabbed my pitcher of ale, which was my job for the night.

"Keep 'em fed and full of drink, Mollie," Iona had told me just before we headed out. "You will recognize some of the faces, but not all. So stay close." I nodded and did as she said. We broke through the large doors and into a great hall. The light spilled forth from the windows and hit the banners that hung proudly from the ceiling. They portrayed the Walsh clan's colors in bold display. I knew much about this clan, how they came from Ireland originally but made their roots here in Scotland. Malcolm was born and bred here and he would end up fighting and dying for his home. Looking around I saw faces that I did indeed recognize. Sir Malcolm always traveled with four men; Declan Wallace, Torren MacAllister, Angus MacAllister, and Connell Kennedy. They were his band of misfits but they were true to his cause and to the cause of saving Scotland. I never once thought anything less of these men, even though I knew their futures. I knew that not too long after the death of Sir Malcolm, The Act of Union between Scotland and England would be signed causing the Scottish parliament to dissolve. They fought for what they thought was a winning battle. Who was I to deny them of that spirit?

Right away I saw Sir Malcolm's wife, Ainsley, sitting at the head table, facing her loyal followers. She smiled beautifully at the men as they each kissed her hand before they too sat to feast. I went to work pouring drink for everyone who had a goblet. The smell of the ale hit me like a brick. It smelled awful. But these drinkers didn't turn it away. Instead they drank it up and asked for more before I could fill their neighbor's glass. I had to hurry to the kitchen for another refill before the crowd got too feisty for more. I grabbed two pitchers this time, trying to be prepared. As I walked out the doors I was back to pouring. I looked back up to the head table, as that was my destination. The lady of the castle got the last glass, as was customary. I stepped up onto the stairs that held her massive wood table.

"Ah, a familiar face," she said as she smiled at me. Ainsley was always nicer than any noble woman I had encountered here. She was once a maid herself before Malcolm married her. He promised himself to her when they were just children and as he told me once, she was to be his bride no matter what. Their story was romantic. He fell in love with her when they were just children.

Ainsley had no children with Malcolm, sadly. Not for lack of trying. She suffered miscarriages and something much worse. Their last child lost at the small age of six months. These times were harsh, which once again reminded me why this wasn't the time for me. Ainsley always had an air of mystery about her. It was told to me by several people that she was special and her heritage had handed her the gift of sight, which in this time period meant she was a seer. In my time period, it meant she may be psychic or faking it; who knows. I didn't really read into it all, I just smiled and nodded.

I bowed to her and replied, "Happy to be back, Milady. Ale?"

She nodded as I poured her the last contents I had in my pitcher. The men behind her had their goblets filled by Iona. "It seems someone forgot to fill my glass," said a man beside Ainsley. His voice was rough around the edges and he sounded upset. I hadn't noticed him before now. Was he there when I filled Ainsley's goblet? If I messed up and she wasn't served last, I could be in trouble with Iona. I didn't understand their ways, but I wouldn't argue at all about the customs they adhered to. This was their house, not mine.

"Oh hush now, you got yours," Iona spoke to the man. I backed up and smiled once more to Ainsley and tried not to be shaken. Why he would try to get me in trouble or to spook me, I wasn't sure. Before I stepped down to the floor, I took a glance at him. I had never seen him with this group before. His long blond hair went almost past his shoulders and didn't fit in much with the other men in the room. His hair was wavy and had a braid that ran through the side of it. His blue eyes and pale skin made him look Nordic, but that voice was very Scottish.

He smiled at Iona and then looked at me with a fierce gaze. He wasn't friendly, that much I knew. I had to find out more about him before I left here. I hurried to the kitchens to prepare for the rest of the feast and tried to keep up with the other girls. Once the dinner was served, Iona had us all eat at a small table in the kitchens.

"Good work tonight, lassies. Lady Ainsley was very pleased with us all. Which reminds me, Mollie, you'll be sleeping here, in the kitchen for the night. Sure that would do you fine. Stay by the fire to stay warm."

I nodded and watched as all the staff dispersed to either clean up or go to their other tasks. I sat down by the fire, surrounded by blankets and watched them like the busy bees they were. I heard a faint song from a faraway distance and wondered if Lady Ainsley had hired a songstress for the evening. When I felt the tug, I knew I was mistaken. Hurrying to a closet, I waited to be pulled back to my time.

****

"You made it back!" Jessa said, her mouth stained with

chocolate. "Here." She handed me a glass of orange juice and took the book from my hands. I drank and let the Vitamin C do its job in restoring my energy. I watched as she cleaned up around us and prepared the room to shut down for the evening. I drained the glass and stood up on wobbly feet. I was back in the blue gown, which threw me for a loop. I thought it would be lost forever.

"What's wrong?" Jessa asked as I hesitated.

"I changed my clothes... and I thought I gave a girl this dress."

Jessa patted me and led me out of the door, shutting the light off behind me.

"This happens every time, remember? You get a little too caught up inside and come out a bit... confused. You're home and your name is not Mollie, it's—"

"Savannah. Yes, it's coming back now. I'm home." Even though I didn't feel like I was really where I belonged, my soul caught up with my body. I was where I needed to be. Home was a word I would never fully come to terms with. Perhaps the mystery of where my dress was, or disappeared to, would find its way to me somehow. But that was the way time travel worked; we didn't always have all the answers.

"You need to get home and rest a little, Savannah. This travel drained you more than the last. Did you find Malcolm, though?"

I shook my head. Defeated.

Four

I woke feeling **renewed and ready** for class. But after my three-class load and my shift at work, I lost all that energy. I didn't want to drive to see my mother, but it was the fifteenth and I promised to go see her. This was a day we usually spent together; if you could call it that. Even if we were fighting, or rather, not speaking currently, I had to see her. The drive home took two hours and it gave me time to think about Malcolm and who the newcomer might have been. Once I pulled into her long cobblestone drive, I had to shut off my brain and prepare myself for the mental torture that was my mother. I parked the car and grabbed my notebook, jotting down my thoughts on Malcolm. I assessed that the newcomer was either Ainsley's brother, lover, or protector. As for Malcolm's whereabouts, I had no clue.

Tuck, my mom's large black lab ambled up to my car, tail wagging with glee. Getting out I pulled him into a hug. His fur was soft and smelled freshly bathed. She was keeping busy, which was a good sign that she was doing well today.

"Oh, you did come after all. I thought you'd forgotten when I didn't hear from you all day long. When the sun set, I gave up all hope." She stood by the porch and watched as Tuck and I walked to the house. I ignored her tone and said, "Hello, Mother. It's the fifteenth, of course I would come. Don't I always?"

She nodded and walked inside the house; not even holding the door for me. I was used to this sort of behavior from her. Especially on this day. It was the worst day.

"Oh, look who it is!" called Laurell, my mom's therapist, from the living room. "Glad to see you. We thought you would forget. It's been an hour, Savannah. You know I'm on your mom's time here and her money is being wasted if you're not here to talk with us."

I hated being chastised for being late. I was in college and I had a job, you'd think they'd give me some slack. Not everyone can drop everything to drive two hours each month.

"I have three classes on Thursday and I work a shift at the library. I've told you both this numerous times," I said, full of sass. Laurell scribbled in her notebook and nodded. "I do remember now. It's been awhile since the fifteenth landed on a Thursday. Forgive me?"

I nodded. "So what did I miss?"

"A lot," snapped my mom. "We were forced to talk about me for an hour." She looked me over and shook her head. "I can see that you haven't been exercising at all. You're back to the weight gain then?"

Biting my tongue, I fought hard to not lash out or defend myself. I had to let what she said roll off. That was harder some days than others. I didn't gain any weight. I was maintaining, if anything. But telling her that would not change her behavior.

Instead I said, "So you talked about you?"

Talking about herself and her issues was the best thing for my mom. She thought this was going to fix us. It wasn't. No matter what, we would never be good. Not because I didn't want it, but more because, there was no fixing her. She was stubborn and angry at my dad for leaving. She never forgave me for that. Her issues didn't need to be mine. But she felt they did. So we met once a month to talk. Nothing ever was resolved. I had come to terms with it.

She just felt better about herself when Laurell left, but never about me. She never forgave me. Tonight, some things were going to change. I was tired of meeting. I was nineteen years old and I had a life to live.

"So, what should we discuss tonight?" asked Laurell. She didn't know about my family or their gift of time travel and she didn't know the real reason my mother hated me so much. It wasn't because I gave up debutant or because she was angry at my dad. Laurell was simply paid to do a service and she did the best she could.

"Let's talk about why I won't be back next month, or the following months after that." I sat down and folded my hands in my lap. I had rehearsed this so many times in my head, but Laurell's face never looked like it did now.

"Here come the theatrics. What's going on in your life that is so important that you can't come see me once a month? Savannah, you know how important therapy is to me."

"To you! Only to you!" I yelled. "It's your issues that you need to work on, Mother. Not mine. I didn't leave you, Dad did. I didn't die, Grandma did. And I didn't take away your destiny. I am not responsible for the natural order of life. But you hate me because the gift wasn't passed down to you."

Her eyes burned with anger and hatred, but I didn't let it scare me. Even though I could feel it steaming off of her.

"What is she talking about?" Laurell asked. We both ignored her.

"You once told me that it was my biggest responsibility and to take it seriously. But then you hate me for it? That makes no sense."

"I don't hate you," she said. "I just don't like you."

I scoffed. Not the first time I had heard that before. I was familiar with her dislike for me.

"Now, Diane, that's not fair to say to Savannah," Laurell told her. "I am not sure what the issue is or what this gift is. I am assuming it's something passed down from your mother?"

My mother nodded. "Yes. You could say that."

It was my gift to travel that made such a wedge between us. Ever since Grandma died, she buried her head in the sand and hated her only daughter. She trained me to be ready for this gift, but when it came, resented me for it.

Laurell told me she didn't hate me once and I knew it to be untrue. Hate blazed in her heart for me. She sure didn't love me. How could you love someone you don't even like?

"Not all mothers love their children," I said to Laurell. "She told me that once you know. It was about a year ago. I had just moved into my new dorm and I called her to talk. She said it to me as if to free herself from her motherly duty. So I stopped calling her for a while. Then she called you. Now on the fifteenth, I'm here to talk about her lack of love for *me*. I don't think I need to be present any longer. Diane is the one who needs therapy. I've come to terms with it. My mom and dad are both gone. I am lost and I am okay with that."

I stood up and paused, waiting for Diane to stop me. She looked away.

"I... I don't know what to say, Savannah." Laurell said honestly. "I can't make you stay here and I can't make you do therapy, because you're saying you don't need it. I think you'd do well with separate sessions, but if you want to go, I understand. Let me walk you out." She grabbed her things and looked at Diane. "You can send your bill. We can work on scheduling *you* twice a month, at my office from now on. I only do house calls for family therapy."

The only thing my mom, Diane, said was, "Fine." She watched us walk out and slammed the door behind us.

Tuck walked me to the car and I wanted to take him with me, but he was probably the only thing Diane loved, so he stayed. "Bye, good dog."

"Savannah, wait a second," Laurell said, grabbing my arm gently. "I can work with her and her issues. You can have your mom back. Her grief is blocking her ability to have feelings right now. It's hard for her to deal with loss, that's apparent. But she does love you. In her way."

I smiled at her. She was trying her best. "I appreciate it, Laurell, I really do. But I don't need her."

Getting into my car and driving away from that house was the hardest thing I ever did, but I didn't regret it one bit. As each tear fell I felt a sense of growth inside me. I stuck up for myself to a woman who never fought for me. I needed to leave this world for a while. I dialed Jessa and told her I needed her.

****

Jessa squeezed me tightly as she met me outside my dorm room. She knew what happened and just knowing that she was there, meant more than anything.

I roomed with her in our dorm, which was more like a luxury apartment. Her parents had money, obviously, and my grandma left me college money. Thankfully Grandma had a large lump of money she'd set aside for me, because Diane didn't help me. Grandma also made sure that the Goode's, Jessa's parents, were there for me. She made them promise to take good care of me if she ever passed. They let me move in with Jessa and tolerated my strangeness because they loved my Grandma so much. Mrs. Goode once pulled me aside and said, point blank, "It's because we cared for Genevieve so much that we felt it was possible that you could share a room with our Jessa. If it wasn't for her, she'd be rooming alone. Or perhaps with that nice Sidney Dolan."

Yeah, I wasn't liked much. But being tolerated was enough for me. Jessa loved me and that's all that mattered. Besides, her folks didn't visit much.

"So, that bad huh?" Jessa asked as she finished getting changed.

I nodded and sucked down the rest of my soda. When I was fighting with Diane I drank and ate junk. Jessa never chastised me for it but there was a certain look she gave me when I walked in carrying the paraphernalia.

"Well, let's go get tacos tonight. I heard Trevor will be there. He switched nights with Clara." She waggled her eyebrows at me and bumped me with her hip. Trevor had worked at Mexican Taqueria for a few months now for side money. It was now my favorite place to eat.

Who could resist seeing Trevor? Not me. I changed

and brushed my stubborn hair and took out my contacts. Switching to glasses was much better since I cried all the way home. Stupid emotions.

My orange tabby cat, Freddy Kruger, came running from Jessa's room and jumped onto my bed. Greeting me for the night before she went to sleep, she ran her body along my black shirt.

"Great, thanks, Fred." I pulled it off and she meowed at me, as if apologizing.

"Wear the teal one," Jessa suggested. "It brings out your brown eyes." She always looked so put together and I was the total opposite. Wrinkled and messy and she was pressed and clean-cut. I used to care, but lately, I wasn't so worried about how I looked. Focusing on Sir Malcolm took up most of my brain function. School wasn't even top priority, which was why I only had three days of classes this year. The rest of the time, I worked and archived. Jessa's major was still undecided, but she was content just taking classes until she figured it out for the past two years. She changed majors three times and drove her parent's nuts. Honestly, I thought she would do something in theatre or even fashion and design, but it took her a long time to come to that realization. I just barely hinted at it a few weeks back and the next day she told me she was changing her major mid-year to theatre.

I dressed in the teal T-shirt and she nodded. Freddy, curled up on my bed, her spot for the rest of the evening, and we left for tacos. While we drove, I filled her in on the nasty details I missed telling her. She cringed when I told her what Diane said.

"Well, one good thing came out of tonight," she said as she parked her Mercedes in the spot nearest the Mexican Taqueria.

"What's that?"

"Diane will have that one-on-one counseling that you said she needed all along. Too bad it took all of this to get her there."

She was right. My mother needed it, and she was getting the help she deserved. I was out and that was all I ever wanted. I wanted to be free and now I was.

"Yeah, I guess. Now, let's stuff our faces and regret it in the morning," I said, pulling her arm. "I'm starving to death."

We walked in and took our seats at the cozy little window table we liked so much. We ordered four tacos each and when they arrived, all steamy and hot, we scarfed them down like ravenous sharks. When the waitress dropped the check at our table with two cute little mints, I looked up and spotted Trevor sitting across the restaurant from us. He wasn't alone, and my heart sank. So much for him working tonight. I tried to see who she was, but it was hard to tell from where I was sitting. I saw she had long blonde hair that curled perfectly at the ends, as opposed to my hair which never held proper curls. She also laughed a lot, another opposite from me. When he reached across the table to tuck her hair behind her ear, I lost it.

"We need to settle the check and leave. Now." I stood up and grabbed my backpack from the table and slung it over my shoulder. Jessa gave me a concerned look and slapped down her half of the check. Tears threatened to fill my eyes, but I stopped them. Either that or I had cried out all that I had on the drive home from Diane's.

"What in the world is going on with you?" Jessa asked as she looked around the room, trying to see what had upset me.

"Hey, Savannah!"

Too late. We had been spotted. Trevor called out to me and I turned his way as he waved, causing his girl to turn to see me. She was drop-dead gorgeous. Of course. Because why would Trevor Arnold want dumpy Savannah? The girl who didn't stand out in crowds and didn't turn heads. You know it wasn't lost on me that I was literally *never* hit on. No one ever turned their head to check me out. And no one asked me out either. I had one boyfriend and I think it was because he wanted practice kissing someone before he left for college.

I closed myself off and left the restaurant without waving back. It was unfair, I know this. But being in that situation, I couldn't wave. I was too sad and too shocked, especially after the day I'd had. I should have known better, really. Did I honestly think that doing his homework for him would get him to like me?

"Savannah! Wait up!" Jessa called as she chased me down. "Girl, you *must* slow down. These heels are not made for running." She gently tugged me back and then pulled me into her arms. "Let it go, girl. Do not let that boy hurt you. You deserve so much—"

"Gah! Save it, Jessa, okay? Did you ever think that boys like that deserve better than me? Huh?"

She let go of me and stepped back like I had wounded her. "Don't ever speak like that again, Savannah Preston! Please don't say things like that about yourself. It hurts my soul to hear that."

I knew it did hurt her, because she loved me. Jessa and I were different people, but we had similar issues with self-esteem. Hers were caused by her parents and mine, well probably the same thing. We just chose to deal with such issues differently.

"Can we go?" I asked, finally, heading for her car.

As we drove away I let the hope of ever being with someone like Trevor Arnold go. I realized he did use me to do his homework. A real friend would have got up and come outside after I left. Or at least called me to see if I was all right. Instead I saw him kissing his girl across the table as if nothing ever happened.

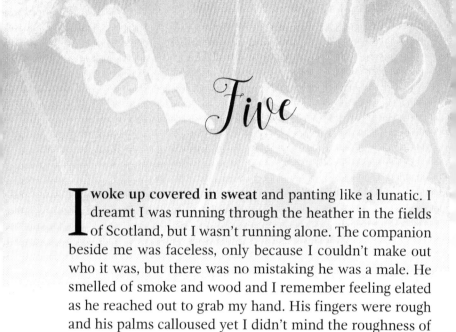

Five

I woke up covered in sweat and panting like a lunatic. I dreamt I was running through the heather in the fields of Scotland, but I wasn't running alone. The companion beside me was faceless, only because I couldn't make out who it was, but there was no mistaking he was a male. He smelled of smoke and wood and I remember feeling elated as he reached out to grab my hand. His fingers were rough and his palms calloused yet I didn't mind the roughness of them. Once we crossed the stream our hands broke apart and he was thrown away from me. Frantically searching for him, I ran through the darkest part of the wood, to no avail. My running partner was gone.

I glanced at the time and saw 4:44 a.m. on my cell phone. After the intensity of the dream I was definitely awake. I swung my legs off the bed, careful not to disturb Fred from her kitty slumber, and walked quietly to the kitchen. After I brewed my coffee, I dressed quietly into some comfortable clothes and my glasses. My eyes were too swollen for contacts today. The need to escape for a little while itched at me. I scratched Fred on her head and left Jessa alone while she got her beauty sleep.

The perfect place for a getaway on the weekend was the campus library; nobody but diehard students would be there. It would be quiet and peaceful. Thankfully traffic was dull at this hour and I got there quickly.

As I entered the library it was just as I thought it would be. The loudest sound was the air-conditioning blowing into the vents above my head as I climbed the stairs to the main entryway. The windows spanned the whole library from top to bottom, letting in tons of natural light. Floors with a colorful pattern brought a certain pop to the old building. The college recently overhauled the library, giving it a more unique and young feel. They added some cool features, like an upstairs studying section that was sound proof and had comfortable white leather chairs and couches. Some students did more than just studying in there, but I wasn't ever one of those people. Jessa on the other hand might have a few stories to share with me about it, but I hardly ever asked her.

I waved to the aid at the desk and headed up the stairs to my favorite section where all the readers would be. They kept to themselves and I could read in peace and quiet. I grabbed a fantasy novel and a soda from the machine and headed to the nearest empty couch.

When I noticed Trevor standing by his new flavor of the week, I halted. He leaned over her as she typed furiously on her laptop. I could see them from behind, and I got a glance at what she was working on. It was a paper on American History, which was his class. Easing a tad closer, I saw it had his name at the top. God! She was doing his homework, too? What was I thinking liking this guy? I was wasting my time and energy on a user, once again.

Avoiding seeing him and making a spectacle like I did

last night forced me to retreat to the basement. I couldn't walk fast enough. My room was a shelter from the sadness and reminder of how different I was here at this school. At least in here I was who I was meant to be. I wasn't Savannah the lost girl, I was the traveler, the archivist. The girl with a destiny to record history. If people really knew what I did, I wondered how they would treat me then. Would teachers still ignore my raised hand as often? Would guys notice me or want to date me? Closing the door behind me helped me to block out the bad thoughts.

I cracked open the book and sniffed it. Sniffing books was so satisfying and albeit weird, but if you were a book lover, you did it. Sitting back and getting comfortable I began reading the first page. It was hard not to travel through a book when I read it. It was entirely possible to travel through books that were fiction, once I started my duty as a Librarian. When I did, it felt like the book was now a movie playing live just for me. Everything was in front of me, close enough to touch, but you knew you shouldn't. I didn't care for it that way, so I usually removed my bracelet and read, the old-fashioned way. But today, I kept it on to practice my skills at reading without moving through the book. That required more focus, but it was important to learn.

A few minutes into the book I heard a sound that made me stop reading and listen. It sounded like music, but there was no music down here, and with the thick flooring above me it was impossible to hear anything from the library.

There it was again, faint but still loud enough for me to pick up on. Listening carefully, I realized it was bagpipes. I put the book down and got up to investigate the sound. It wasn't coming from outside, so I stopped and listened with my eyes closed. It was in the room somewhere. Not my cell phone, I had checked that. When I got close to where we hid the book I was currently traveling through, the sound got louder and louder. I pulled it free from its hiding spot and it was vibrating with the sound of Scottish bagpipes playing a melodious tune.

Absentmindedly opening the book, I turned to the page I was last on, to see what the devil was going on. Before I knew it, I was being pulled into the book, even as I tried to hold onto the present time, I realized it was hopeless. I was going in whether I wanted to or not.

I blinked to clear my eyes from the tears that blurred my vision. I had lost control of my surroundings and for some reason, I was face down in the foulest smelling room. The tears were not those of sadness, but rather from pain and stench. I pushed my arms up, hoping to rise, but my back screamed in pain. I tried to imagine what could have happened between the time I was in the library and now, but I came up blank. I had lost time and was completely confused, which was not usual for me. I turned my face and looked around to see where I was, but it was dark. I fumbled for my glasses and found them underneath me, still intact, or so it seemed in the dark room. Leaning on my other senses, I used my hands to feel around me. The ground was solid dirt with some straw. My hands felt something squishy and hot, and I knew instantly that it was horse droppings. I gagged and rolled my body away from it and came face to face with a mare. She blew her nose at me and neighed.

"Gee, thanks," I told her. At least now I knew where I was and who was around me. I wasn't in the dungeons at least. Being surrounded by horses was better than coming here unexpectedly and having to explain my current attire to an unsuspecting maid.

The horse leaned her head down and nibbled on my belly and I recognized her companion beside her as Frith. "What's your name, huh?" I asked petting her nose. I had to get up and wash the dirt from my body. I pulled myself upright using the mare's head for support.

Once I got to my feet, I assessed my bodily situation. My back was aching and my knees bloody. I had fallen, no doubt, and probably knocked unconscious from my fall. I hoped no one had seen me lying here, but I wholly doubted it. My eyes adjusted to the darkness and the moon shone in through the open stable door, giving off just enough light to see around me.

Washing my hands in a clean trough, I looked around to see if anyone was nearby. It seemed quiet, quiet enough to sneak out, but my plans after that were dim. I needed clothes but getting them and not being spotted was going to be hard. I leaned against the wood of the stall entryway, hiding from any prying eyes, and wondered why the hell I was here. Did the book call to me? If so, why? Nothing like this has ever happened in the history of the Librarians. I would know, because I've studied the logs thousands of times as a young girl. If it did happen, no one spoke about it. I did learn of librarians who chose to stay inside the books, and the outcome was always disastrous.

It would change the course of history, and the target would not do what they set out to. But a book calling to a traveler just didn't make sense. I pondered why it would happen while I watched the dark for any signs of movement.

The shock of being tossed here had kept my mind away from Jessa, but as I stood there in the silence of the night, it all came crashing down. Jessa would be panicked, beyond belief. But once the book was through with me, and sent me back, I could explain to her this strange occurrence. I stretched my back and felt a lovely crack which made it feel better, but that didn't help my bloody knees. Finding some clean rags, I wrapped them and cleaned off the blood.

"Hey, you there! What business do you have with these horses?" I swung around, terrified of what I might find. I had been so busy watching the outside that I didn't focus on the inside. A portly man in his later years studied me as I held up my hand.

"I mean no harm. I am from the kitchens. I merely came here to see the mares," I lied, with ease.

He came closer, holding out a stick and staring at me sideways. "Ah, from the kitchens are ye? Well, then go back to them, you've no business here, these are my horses."

I didn't know what to say next. I couldn't explain to him that I was waiting for the coast to be clear so I could sneak inside and get clothes. I had to stall somehow.

"I think I injured myself on the way in. I twisted my leg so I thought I'd rest for a minute before I tried to walk on it again." Lying became so easy now that sometimes I forgot how many I've told.

He backed up a bit and held out his stick. "I can't be helping ye. I've not got the eyes for it. I'm almost blind already. The last battle took most of what I had, and that wasn't much."

So he was partially blind then. It did work to my advantage even though it was tragic. He couldn't see me properly, nor could he see just how much I currently did not fit in with the time period.

"I'll be out of your stalls before you know it. I don't need anything besides a small bit of rest. Once my leg is better I'll make my way to the kitchens."

He scoffed. "Och, aye, you will. You'll be making your way there before Iona finds out you're here and tans my hide for keeping a young girl in my stables. I'll not have any suspicion with her."

I was confused of his meaning, but I nodded anyway; which was stupid because it wasn't like he saw me.

"You stay here and I'll go off to bed. Don't touch anything." He grumpily walked away and I said goodbye to the horsemaster. Now that I met him, I knew why the horses looked so thin and in such rough shape; he couldn't see how awful they looked. Once he was out of sight, I fed them myself and gave them each a good brushing. Except for the horse on the end. That black mare was antsy and I didn't care to really injure myself.

I kept waiting for the soldiers outside to leave their posts, but it didn't happen during the night. It wasn't until early dawn that they finally left and I had my chance to run inside. As soundlessly as possible, I ran across the empty courtyard and into the doors of the castle that I had entered into on my first arrival here. I found myself in Marsen's quarters and searched for the kitchen attire I needed. With my arms full, I dressed in the proper undergarments, including a pair of heavy wool stockings that would keep my legs nice and warm in this drafty cold castle. The brown overdress hung tightly over my curves but looked less restricting when I applied my loose apron. The shoes were another issue indeed. They were odd fitting and the strangest thing to get used to when you normally wore sandals or sneakers, but they were easy to slip on. I reached up to my glasses and took them off my face. I could see a little bit without them, but I saw best with them on. I could go without and

I knew, to fit in here that I'd have to. I tucked them inside my clothes and into a leather satchel.

Once dressed, I quietly left the room and headed for the kitchens and the area that Iona had told me was mine for the night. The fire was lit and warm, and the rug that served as a bed was empty. I laid down and stared at the dying flames of the fire, trying to think of a good reason to tell Iona why I was missing. When I left I had no idea how many days, months or hours could have passed. The only way to know, really know, was to return and deal with the consequences. I usually had a good story, like last time, but this time was different. I was already away from these people for so long, that suspicion would surely grow. They were hiding out here in this castle; this fortress. Sir Malcolm wasn't here to protect them from the English if they stumbled upon this site. His wife and all of her people would surely be slaughtered.

I couldn't raise alarm, for fear of them throwing me in the stocks or outright killing me. I had to find Sir Malcolm, but the stupid book kept bringing me back here, for some reason or another. Perhaps Sir Malcolm was here, somewhere close, hiding. If that were so, he was hiding very well. As I rolled onto my other side I reached up to push my bracelet up higher, so it wasn't seen by anyone's prying eyes. When my hand touched nothing but skin, I sucked in a deep breath. My bracelet was gone!

Six

I panicked silently, hoping that the muffled sound of my crying wouldn't wake anyone sleeping near the kitchen. I retraced my steps from the stables, even risking being seen by guards, but found nothing. Now as I sat on the rug by the cold fire, I cried and worried. There was nothing else to do but hope it turned up when I could get a better look. The sun was already coming up and looking in the dim moonlight was impossible. Once the sun arose I would find it for sure. That is if someone else didn't find it first.

Oh, no, this was terrible. The bracelet was my only way back home and I was screwed without it. If someone found it, I may never see it again. The rose gold color of the bracelet would catch someone a pretty penny if sold. My grandmother had a safety latch put on the clasp, preventing breakage, and hadn't ever lost it before me. I *had* to be the one to lose such an important family artifact. Burying my face, I sobbed even harder.

"Why Mollie, whatever is the matter, love?" Asked a very sleepy Iona. I looked up to see her concerned face and wanted nothing more than to run into her arms. Iona was such a lovely person, and her caring soul was hard to find in my time.

"I've lost something important, Iona," I cried softly. "I am afraid it's going to be gone forever."

She sat next to me and put her hand on my shoulder, "No, my sweet, you'll find it again. When you truly stop looking for it, it will return to you. You'll see. Now, get yourself up and help me get breakfast ready for everyone. Today is a calm day, you know the sort. No fussing about, just regular meals for all. Then you can help stock the pantry, as is your job now. And then you will find what you've lost."

I sniffed. "You're not concerned that I was gone, are you?"

She waved her hands and said, "Bah, no. We've gone over it. You're back now and that's all that matters. You get to start your first day back here with us. We've all missed you so. Well, me more than anyone else, really."

So I came back on the very night I had left before. I had arrived in sync with their time period. How strange. But then everything about this travel was different. I was called here and now I was stuck here. Perfect.

I set about helping Iona with breakfast and even helped them set up the feast in the hall. When they ate in the morning, they had it buffet style. Although, they didn't call it that, they usually ate that way unless it was a special occasion. Serving them anything besides ale, wine, or whiskey would be rare. But my job was in the pantry now, keeping it stocked and making sure the castle had the correct amount of food to keep everyone fed. As I set about to do that, I worried my lower lip wondering how long I would be stuck here. If I didn't find my bracelet, my way home, it would be forever. I would never go home. Oh geez, that couldn't happen. Staying in this century would be absolute madness. The future for Scotland was increasingly grim. Once Robert the Bruce became king, it would be better for a while. But then the fighting would start again. Well, it never really stopped until they gained their freedom. As I oversaw what was already in the pantry, I came across something smelling just like chocolate, and as I pulled it out saw that it was an herb. Of course chocolate wasn't a food source in Scotland just yet, but the herb smelled amazing. As I put it to my nose, the smell reminded me of Jessa and her chocolate covered face. I put the bottle back, trying hard not to think of how worried she must be right now. What would happen to my life back home if I went missing for years? Would Jessa know where I was, or would she think that I ran away? I sighed and continued my work as fast as I could so I could go out and look for my bracelet.

Placing the last item on the shelf, I ran out to the courtyard, where men were training for battle and women were watching in awe. I rolled my eyes, trying to focus on my mission, choosing to ignore the kilt wearing men. I found nothing in the courtyard, so I returned to the stables.

"Hello," I called, to the horsemaster. "It's me, um, Mollie from last night. I seem to have dropped something and I came to look for it."

Silence. He wasn't here or he was sleeping still, which was entirely possible. I entered anyhow and ran my hands along the wood, petting the horses as their noses poked out of their stalls. I found the stall for the horse that I had met with last night when I came crashing in. I opened her stall door and found it empty, horse and all was gone. Even her feed and manure had been cleaned out.

Hearing a sound behind me, I ran out of the stall, I had to find out who had it cleaned. They may have my bracelet.

"Hello! I need to talk to you," I said to the sound in the back of the stable. When the sun poked through the clouds, and the stable filled with brilliant light, I saw that the sound wasn't coming from the horsemaster, but from a large blond Scotsman who was brushing the black stallion that I didn't dare touch. He stopped brushing as I neared and then finally turned to face me.

He was the man from last night's feast. The stranger I had never seen before. His angry face, faced mine and he threw his brush to the ground.

"What are you doing in here? Don't you know that kitchen maids stay in the bloody kitchen?"

When he spoke he spat, and I could see pure hatred in his blue eyes. I couldn't imagine what would cause a man to hate a girl he didn't know so much, but I backed up, not wishing to find out.

"I apologize, I was looking for something very dear to me and I came to see if it was here. That's all."

He scoffed and said, "There is nothing here of yours, wench. Now be gone before I shove you out."

"Of course," I bit out, trying not to cry. As I turned around I said as low as I could under my breath, "Bastard."

"What did you call me?" I froze, not so much because he heard me, but because I had said it in English, not Gaelic, and he had understood me. Most of the people in Sir Malcolm's household and the people that swore their fealty to him spoke in Gaelic, the language of the Scots. Some spoke in English, but it was rare.

Before I knew it, he was grabbing me and turning me to face him. "Don't ye ever call me that. Do ye hear me? I will not be talked to like that by some... some traitorous sneaking spy! Calling me a bastard is like me calling you a... a whore! It isn't right."

I ripped myself free and fought the tears that came fast. "How dare you! I am not a whore, I am a lady. I've done nothing to you, but you treat me so ugly. You truly *are* a bastard and I will not take it back."

He huffed and growled and that scared me more than his words. He was seriously angry with me for no apparent reason. He only shook his head at me instead of apologizing.

"Why do you dislike me so much? I need help looking for something and you are so mean to me. Why? What did I ever do to you?" I asked as tears poured out of my eyes. I wanted to run away so badly, but I needed to find my bracelet more than I needed to get out of there. I would stay here until I had answers.

"I don't trust you, is why I don't like you. I've never seen you before and you've that look about you that tells me you are not who you say you are. Mollie. Mollie what? From where?"

I swallowed hard. I had a backstory, and I knew it well, but as I stood before this man, I found it hard to remember.

"Mollie Wallace from Aberdeenshire. I came here with Iona, when she decided to follow Mistress Ainsley into hiding. I've met with Sir Malcolm many times and have been with his men and his followers for a year now. I've fallen ill and had to stay away for a time, but I am back. And I must say," I said, calmly, "I've never seen you before now. So who exactly are you, huh?"

"Who I am, is none of your concern, Mollie Wallace from Aberdeenshire. I know my place in this castle and it's to fight, not to play with kitchen maids."

Oh my God he was so frustrating. If I could slap him, I would. But his height must have been about six foot six, way taller than my tiny five foot four. He towered over me and his muscle mass dwarfed me. Regardless of his size, I refused to let him call me a whore.

"You are an angry person, whoever you are. And it wasn't right that you called me that ugly word. If you were a real man you'd take that back and apologize to me. But you won't do that, will you? Now please tell me, what happened to the mare in that stall?" I said, pointing to her empty stall. "And who cleaned it out?"

He peered into the stall and then looked at me and shrugged. "Don't know. How ya see the stall is how I saw it when I arrived."

That didn't add up. I left here not too long before sunrise, and she was fine when I left.

"Then who was here before you?"

"The horsemaster was, but he's still asleep. Sorry that I can't help you. What is it you're looking for then?"

I wouldn't be giving him the satisfaction of knowing what I had lost. Screw that! I turned on my heel and marched out of the stables and went in search for the mare. If she was with a rider then surely they would know who cleaned the stall out. An hour later I found her out in the pasture eating grass and her rider was Lady Ainsley. As I came upon her, I bowed my head and greeted her. Seems she wanted a ride with her best horse.

"I know the conditions of the stables, Mollie," she told me as she watched the horse feed. "I had Eoin clean out her stall this morning. She deserves to be free today and not be locked up. I suppose we all want a little freedom, lately."

Eoin. So now I knew the name of the man or boy I had to track down. I watched the horse with Ainsley for a while and then before it got too late, dismissed myself. It was better that I did anyway, she was looking a bit sad and I didn't want to bother her any longer than I already had.

I had a mission now, to find Eoin and get my bracelet

back. My luck would be he was a thieving child who already sold it. As I set my eyes back on the castle the supper horn was ringing and I knew I had to hurry to clean up. Dinner would be served soon and I was expected to play my role here for now. It wouldn't be long. I would find my ticket back home and then I would stop traveling until I found out why the book did what it did. Finding answers would mean taking a trip to visit with some other librarians who might know better than I. Finding Sir Malcolm might never happen. His story may never have a real ending, but right now I didn't care about that. All I cared about was getting home.

****

The dinner rush swallowed up my whole night. I was spent by the time we were finished in the kitchen and I had zero energy to search the castle for this Eoin. At least my mind had been on other things, instead of the dread of being stuck here. After helping the ladies in the kitchen clean up, I took off my apron and hung it in the pantry. It was fully stocked and ready for the next day, so I took my leave. I finally had some time to investigate. Hopefully I could be sneaky enough and no one would question why I was wandering about the castle at night. It seemed everyone was on edge lately. In the past, whenever I would come here and visit with Sir Malcolm, I'd see happy cheerful Scots. This time, though, they were not as merry. Maybe it was because the state of their country, or because Sir Malcolm had to go into hiding. I knew with Ainsley it had to be that he was gone. If I had loved someone like she loved him, I'd feel the same way. But the castle as a whole was hushed and secretive. I mean just today I was thought to be a spy, and no one trusted anyone it seemed. During dinner a fight had broken out between Torren MacAllister and Connell Kennedy over something, I wasn't sure what. But it was odd to see them fighting because these men were part of Sir Malcolm's band of warriors. They fought together for Scotland's rights and freedom and they shouldn't be fighting each other.

As I came out of the kitchens I passed a man and a woman in the shadows sneaking nighttime kisses that would lead to goodness knows what. I climbed the first set of steps that led me out into the main floor. I hadn't explored the castle yet and doing so now was perfect because things were quiet and calm. Most everyone was drunken by the wine served at dinner or doing so with whiskey in their own personal rooms. I didn't care for the Scottish whiskey myself. It was entirely too strong, so I always held up a hand and politely said no. The main floor was lit so beautifully with candles that the shadows literally seemed to dance upon the stone walls as I walked. I would never get used to how different things were in medieval times. I wasn't able to use a bathroom with indoor plumbing until I got back, and it was awful. I tried to grin and bear it but the thought of not being able to have privacy for the rest of my time here was rough. I would have to bathe at some point and that would kill me. Bathing wasn't something that a lot of people felt necessary to do on a regular basis. When they did they usually would do so in the bath house, which in this castle seemed to be located right outside the kitchen, by the main garden. As I went outside earlier to fill up my spices, I saw naked men washing themselves in a small building. The doors were open, and in the center of the room there was a pool of water that they were climbing in and out of. I had never seen anything like it before.

When I asked Iona what the room was for she

chuckled and told me that it was the bathing house. I must have gone white when she told me our wash day was in three days. She had patted my shoulder and said, "Oh, it's alright, love. You just go in and wash up and then it's over. You'll see, it's easy. No reason to fret. And then you don't have to do it for another two weeks"

I had never had to bathe here before, because I'd never stayed long enough to get dirty. I'm sure there was a nearby lake I could use instead of the bath house. I was not, and I mean not, bathing in front of a bunch of strangers. Seeing this body naked would likely shock a lot of people, and it wasn't something I was ever comfortable with. No one besides my mother had seen me nude before. Being comfortable in my own skin was a goal I had someday, but it wouldn't happen here. Jessa always walked around in her underwear, and I could never understand it. She said once that it made her feel free. Feeling free was something totally different for me. That would leave me feeling totally exposed.

As I continued walking, it seemed as if the castle went on and on. It was rather huge. Not sure where I was going, I knew not to go upstairs, because that's where the personal bedrooms were. I meant to stay on this floor and to explore as much as I could until I found my way around. And once that was done, I would find this boy that I was searching for. But once I reached the far eastern part of the corner I stopped dead in my tracks. I had found something I never thought possible in this era, a library.

Seven

Most castles in this era didn't have need for libraries, since they were meant for military purposes. So as I stepped inside the room that held so many books before me, I was shocked. Pleased, but shocked. The room wasn't huge by any means, but it was still by all accounts, a library. The large stone fireplace was burning low and it was a tad bit cold in here. I stoked the fire with the poker to help the logs burn longer. But it didn't seem to help at all. The flames were still small when I heard a large voice behind me say, "Ye might want to try to add another log to it. Or using this." He reached around me and took a tool to add a blast of air to the dying fire. This made the fire blaze and his breath on my neck caused the hair on my arms to stand on end and gave me chills. I remained frozen as he added a log to the fireplace. I wasn't supposed to be in rooms such as these and if this person was one of Sir Malcolm's fighters, I could be in serious trouble. I didn't want to get locked up in the dungeon. I had heard the horror stories from the other servants about the conditions of it. I did hear that there was an Englishman locked down there who wouldn't likely see the light of day anytime soon.

"Lass, you may get up. Unless you like kneeling by the fire like so," he said. I stood slowly and turned around. It was the guy from the stables. His face looked kinder, maybe because it was clean. His blond hair pulled all the way back and tied with a piece of leather. I had to leave.

"If you'll excuse me, sir. I'll take my leave. I must be off to bed," I said as I tried to duck around him.

"Oh, no you don't lass. What are ye doing in this room, then?"

I swallowed hard. "I came to check on the fire."

He shook his head. "Is everything you say a lie? Do you ever say the truth?"

How did he know I was lying to him? What was it about me that showed him my lies?

"I was checking the fire. What are *you* doing in here?"

I realized then that we were both speaking English and not Gaelic. I had something on him.

"And how do you know English?" I had acquired the correct dialect and accent by now, so I sounded Scottish as well. It wasn't hard to do, but it was hard when you were scared or frustrated, like I often was.

"Why do you?"

"Because I do, that's why. Now may I leave?" I asked pointing to the doorway.

He stood tall and said, "No. Ye can't leave."

Great! I was stuck in here with this brute at the farthest end of the castle where no one would likely hear me. I stepped back, away from him and tried to look for a way out of this.

"I'll scream," I said, foolishly.

He looked at me funny and then started laughing. His

laugh was hardy and almost made me laugh with him. It didn't match his personality at all. I wondered what his deal was. What his story really was, because he was mysterious indeed.

"I mean to tell you something," he said, reaching behind him. He slowly pulled something from his back and I braced myself, expecting a blade to flash at me at any moment. I had no weapon to protect myself with.

When I looked down I saw the poker and knew that was what I needed to get. So I bent down and reached for it as quickly as I could. When I looked up, I came face to face with what he was pulling out; a beautiful purple flower.

"I picked this for ye, lass. After our encounter today in the stables, I felt awful. I went out on a walk, to calm my head, you see. And I came across a field of the most beautiful thistles you could ever find. It's hard to find them here, especially when it's getting cold. I shouldn't have said that word to you. I never meant to call you that. I only meant to say that calling me a bastard was *the same as* me calling you that. That's not what you are. I know that."

Wow. What a strange turn around. I stood up, awkwardly dropping the poker, and took the thistle. It *was* beautiful. I had never seen one up close before. The sharp sections of the flower were odd, but the beautiful petals at the top made up for its strangeness. The vibrant purple was my favorite color. The flower was unique, like me.

I sniffed it and realized the scent wasn't my favorite, but the flower was gorgeous and the thought behind it even better.

"Thank you. Apology accepted."

He nodded, but still didn't smile. It made me wonder if he had the ability to do so. Maybe being in this castle had that effect on people. The dank smell coupled with the feeling that you were locked inside a crypt didn't help my attitude that was for sure.

"I am sorry for calling you a bastard. I didn't know it would strike such a nerve. I just wanted to find the boy who mucked the stall out. I lost something and you... you made that difficult for me. I got angry," I said as I tucked the thistle into my apron. "By the way, do you know where I can find him?"

"Find who?"

"Eoin. Mistress Ainsley said he's the one who cleaned the stall."

His face turned red and then I saw it. A smile; cocky yet clever. "Och, aye. That's me."

Eight

Of course that was him. Well, at least this guy had a name though. But now I was stuck at another dead-end road. He already said he didn't find my bracelet. It made me wonder if I had lost it somewhere else, but in the back of my mind, I knew it was gone. And that meant, I was here forever now.

I moved toward the wooden chair in the room and sat down with a thud. My head in my hands, I couldn't help but weep, loudly. Eoin didn't move or say a word. But he didn't leave. I cried so hard snot began to pour out and when Eoin handed me a handkerchief, I thanked him with a nod of my head. I looked up and saw him staring at the flames and letting me do my thing. He was an odd guy. He seemed quiet and reserved and very mysterious. After a few minutes, I calmed myself slowly. Eoin sat in the adjacent seat and pulled out a blade from his belt. He began to whittle a small piece of wood from the pile near the fireplace. We sat like that in silence for a while. Neither of us talking, just sitting there. I pulled a book from the only shelf near me and thumbed through the pages.

"Not sure if you should be reading Mistress's books, lass," Eoin said finally. He was right. I put it back carefully.

"I love books. I can't help myself," I told him. "Do you carve wood frequently?" It was a strange conversation starter, but given the moment, I had nothing else.

He blew the wood chips off of his kilt and nodded.

"Aye. It helps pass the time. When you are alone, like I was, it's the one thing you get good at doing. I have many pieces carved. I used to sell them where I came from. I had many customers who would request different pieces; a dog, a flower, and even toys. When my ma became ill I stopped to take care of her. But then she died, and I took it up again."

Wow. That was more information than I expected him to give me.

"Sorry to hear about your mother. Did you have a good relationship with her?"

He nodded and then looked up at me. "Why? Don't you have a good one with your ma?"

"Not my favorite thing to speak about. Tell me about your father." I wiped my nose and tried to hand him back the hanky.

"Ah, keep it. I have more," he said, holding up a hand. "My da. He was brave, strong, and pigheaded. But he wasn't around much. He's married, not to my ma. So when you called me a bastard, you weren't far from the truth."

Oh crud. Of course I would screw something like that up. I felt horrible now. Me and my mouth.

"Sorry."

He shrugged and then went back to carving. I wondered how long we were going to sit there in one another's company. Would he eventually get up and leave, or was he waiting on me?

"Oh, heaven's me." Eoin and I both looked up to see

Mistress Ainsley crossing the threshold. "I certainly didn't think to see anyone in here at this late hour."

She was dressed in her night robe and her golden hair was down around her shoulders. She looked like an angel.

I stood fast and bowed to her. "Mistress, I am just leaving. I came in here to check the fire. And then Eoin—"

"No need to apologize, Mollie. 'Tis all right. I am glad that I found you, though, my dear. I am in need of assistance in my room, if that's not a bother. I know that you are working in the pantry, but my clothier and maid are both ill at the moment. It seems that there is something taking all of my help and making them sick. I saw two others disposing of their stomach contents earlier." She made a face of disgust and I tried hard not to laugh. I just thought briefly of the last time Jessa got drunk. What a big mistake that was. She cannot handle her liquor at all! She puked from one end of our apartment to the other. Ainsley would have had a heart attack at that sight. "Is that something you can help me with?"

I nodded, breaking my thought of Jessa. "Of course, Mistress. Anything to assist you."

"Very well. Grab me a book and follow me." I looked for the book I just had and pulled it free once more. Ainsley took leave and I followed. Just before I left the room, Eoin touched my hand.

"Find me tomorrow," he whispered. Chills ran through me and I found myself nodding like a silly schoolgirl. We locked eyes and for a brief moment, for that one second, I didn't feel lost. When I blinked, it was over.

Ainsley's quarters were massive. They spanned one whole length of the east side of the castle. They held a personal bathroom, which was quant for my taste, but in this era extravagant, and a bedroom so large it tripled mine. Her bed was made from real wood and was draped in white cloth around the four posts. The quilt was no doubt real Scotch wool and the color was a deep blue and red. I thought about the ways they would have had to dye the wool to get such colors in this time; it was magnificently rich.

"Do you like my bed?" she asked as she began to undress. Things were getting awkward fast. I wasn't sure what she needed me for, but it seemed like she didn't need my assistance taking her clothes off.

"Err, of course. It's very pretty, Mistress."

She nodded and turned so that her back faced me. "I need help, with the laces," she clarified, finally. I began working on them and she breathed a sigh of relief. I understood what she felt, for I too was in pain due to the clothes I wore. Once she was unlaced, I pulled off her corset and helped her step out of it. Standing in just her shift, she faced me. "Can you fill the tub with water? It will need warming in the fireplace."

I turned to the fire, and then to the tub. "I know, my dear. It's strange that I bathe this often, but it comforts me when my husband is away. I do love to soak in the tub."

Who was I to ask questions or assume something was odd? I showered daily at home. My hesitation wasn't on the frequency of her bathing, but the method. This was going to take forever. I nodded my head and went to work heating the water on the fire. I had no idea how to do it, but after watching Iona do it daily in the kitchens, I was learning fast.

"Are your da and ma still alive, Mollie?"

I swallowed hard, not sure how to answer, so I decided for honesty.

"My mother is still alive, yes. We have a hard relationship. We grew apart. As for my father, he is married to another woman. I guess you could say I never knew him well."

"Ah, aye. My ma and I are not close at all. And my da is dead, seven long years now. Seems everyone dies when you don't want them to. Are you wanting marriage soon?"

It wasn't unusual for her to ask me this. Women in this time were usually married by my age. I was actually considered too old to be single. At nineteen most girls were already married with one or two babies, or bairns as they referred to them.

"Your water is warm enough, now," I said, avoiding the answer. I turned around and Ainsley was already in the large tub, awaiting the water. I poured it in slowly and she lay back relaxing. I heated two more pots full of warm water, and Ainsley told me that I could ready her bed while she soaked.

I made it up the way I would make my own, hoping that it would suit her needs. When she was ready to get out, I helped her into her shift and into bed. Before I pulled the covers over her she grabbed my hand gently.

"Sit with me awhile. It would be nice to have a bit of company before I drift off to sleep," she said. "Will you read to me a bit?"

I sat beside the bed in a small wooden chair and opened the book. I read aloud to her which was hard to do without my glasses in the dim light. After the first couple of pages she interrupted me. I was thankful because reading Gaelic was a horrid business. I could speak it fluently, but reading it was like reading scrambled words. She must have thought me unable to read, because she told me I didn't have to. It would suit my position to be illiterate I suppose.

"Why are ya here, Mollie? Why not with your family or married off? You're bonnie enough for a fine husband."

I shrugged. I wasn't pretty enough for a fine anything back home. Here, I guess I blended in with the other ladies in the kitchen, but I would never consider myself a catch.

"I like it here," was my answer.

"There is something keeping you here, is that it?"

I nodded. "Something like that."

"Maybe a calling, or you're stuck. I can't really tell which it is. But it is certain you are not meant to be here, lassie. That I can see as plain as the nose on your face."

Sitting back hard in my chair, shock overcame me. I never put much thought to the rumors that went around about Lady Ainsley having the 'gift of sight.' Most people didn't believe in seers, but then again, no one thought time-travel was possible either. I was here to prove that it was.

"Do ya want to leave?" she asked, simply. I decided to go with it and answer honestly; as honestly as I could.

"I lost something very important to me," I began. "It is the reason I am here at all, really. The problem is that I cannot find it and I think someone found it and sold it. I cannot leave until I have it back in my possession. Then I can go home, for good. I guess my time here is over after that."

"Did ya lose it in the stables? Is that why you were so frantic that day?"

"Yes, I did. Eoin hasn't seen it but he was the only one in there that day. I just need to have it back." Tears came fast and I was embarrassed to cry in front of her but too tired to fight them off. In the end they won and I was a blubbering mess. I sniffed loudly and remembered the handkerchief Eoin had given me. Pulling it out, I wiped my mess of a face.

"If you find it, will you leave and go back home where you belong? Do you promise me that, Mollie?"

Why was it so important to her that I promised her?

"I promise," I said. "Do you not want me here?"

She shook her head and patted my hand gently. "Och, no! Of course I want you here, Mollie, but you see, you don't belong here, do ya?"

I only stared at her in awe. How she knew I didn't belong here was beyond me.

"But you don't belong anywhere now do you? Now that one is twisty. You are truly lost, aren't you?"

Nine

I **didn't belong back at home.** I had felt it a million times and more. And Ainsley was right, I didn't belong anywhere. My sense of self did not feel whole. Maybe it was because of my relationship with Diane, or maybe it was just me. Perhaps it was because my dad left me to live with someone else and start fresh. Shoot, maybe I didn't get along with my mom because I was a bad person who did horrible, mean things. I could possibly have some issues myself that needed help. You'd think after intense therapy I would have hashed all that out, though, right?

Soon after Ainsley said those words the tears stopped and she sat up in her bed.

"I think I know what you need," she said. I sat on the edge of the chair intently listening. Whatever she said I would do. I was literally stuck here with my mission incomplete and the fate of my very life hanging in the balance. I wouldn't find Sir Malcolm, until I found myself. There was no doubt that I had failed already. Who knew where he was? I wasn't going to try to find out. I had to get back to my time and figure out some things about me first.

I had been diving into these books for so long that I had forgotten *me*. Forgotten what was important.

The duty of being a Librarian was ingrained in me at such a young age, that that was all I thought I needed. But take away your freedom, and all that is familiar and that doesn't seem so important anymore. Sure, my duty to serve as Librarian was still something I wanted, but if I didn't know who I really was as a person, then I needed to fix that. I would always have the gift that would never change.

"You need someone to watch over you, first and foremost. Then, when you've someone you trust, you take yourself into the stables and find a fine horse. Ride two days south, until you reach the first village. Ask them about what you've lost. If they don't know, then stop looking."

I sucked in a sharp breath. That's it?

"But... but how could I give up after only one town? I'd be stuck here," I exclaimed.

She shrugged. "Mollie, if they haven't this item in that village, then it is gone for good. That is the nearest town for trade. You won't find another any closer. If it hasn't been traded there, then you'll never find it again. It left you for a reason."

"What reason could my bracelet have for up and walking away? Or for someone stealing it? Being stuck here forever isn't an option."

She smiled at me. "It can't be all that bad, can it? I will house you here in this fine castle. I'll even find you a husband if you wish it."

I stood up, angry now. Those couldn't be my only options.

"You don't understand, Ainsley. I must get home," I cried. "I have a friend who's probably worried sick about me. I have a life. I can't be stuck here forever living as a pantry maid. You say I don't belong here, and that I may not belong back at home. Well, where do I belong, huh?"

She yawned, as if my rant bored her.

"I'm tired lass. You'll best be going now. I need my sleep. And you will find your answers when you leave, next week. Now, be gone with you, lassie. Do as I said. But make sure you find a trustworthy protector. I want you to have a good plan in place before you leave."

And with that she lay down and rolled over. My mouth remained hanging open, but I took my leave of her quarters. As I walked down the stairs to the main floor of the castle, I felt like I was in a fog. Exhaustion overcame me so I found my spot near the fireplace and fell in a heap. I didn't even have a room here, or a bed. The tears were still falling down my face when the fire went out. I must have been crying for hours. I silently rubbed the thistle, finding some comfort in one act of kindness.

Tissues by that point were something I realized I missed dearly, as snot just poured out and the hanky was no longer helping. I realized it was useless to fight sleep, so I closed my eyes and drifted off.

****

I worked the one week needed, until Ainsley gave me my official permission to leave the castle and go to town to find my bracelet. Days and weeks blended together here. I had lost count by week two and began fitting into the Scottish traditions fast. It was either that or someone discover that I didn't belong here. I stayed in the kitchens and mostly in my pantry, stocking and keeping it tidy. During the night I served the inhabitants of the castle, staying far away from anyone who gave me ill looks. If I stayed quiet and busy, no one would notice me here.

Lady Ainsley was to hold a feast for her people in celebration of the coming moon on my last night in the castle. To prepare for such a feast of epic proportions Iona needed all hands on deck. All of us servants and kitchen staff had jobs tending to the food and to the decor of the castle. According to Iona, Lady Ainsley celebrated the first full moon of every month, in the hopes of her husband's return. Perhaps she hoped he'd find his way home by the light of the moon, I wasn't sure. And it was no ordinary feast. The men went out the day before to hunt wild boar, a dangerous business, and we did our jobs. I had heard that the best hunter for boar was Eoin. Alaire, a handmaid, sat back against the stone wall of the kitchen to tell us all about how Eoin killed the last boar.

I worked and listened, trying hard to not look interested, even though I sort of was.

"He saw the boar, but the evil pig didn't see him, ye see. He crouched down, real low, and snuck up on it. But the scent is what gave him away, and the boar turnt around, and ran toward Eoin, almost sticking its tusk into his leg. That would have bled him dry."

Her wild boar tale went on and on keeping all the women in awe up until the very end.

"Then, with a single blow, Eoin stabbed the boar straight across the throat killing it almost instantly."

They all sighed, and I swear some of them fanned themselves. Eoin was popular among the women here. That was plain to see, but he seemed so quiet toward them all, and it dawned on me that it was always the mysterious types that drew in the ladies.

"This boar was killed by Connell Kennedy," Iona stated, as she threw a slab of the meat onto the table. "Do ye have any wild fantastic stories about Connell then?" she asked Alaire.

Alaire just grinned and said, "No."

"Then get yer arse out of my kitchen and go find something to do."

Alaire scoffed and turned around, stomping out the door.

We began working on tenderizing the meat and cooking the vegetables on hand. When everything was done, we served everyone the feast. They all seemed to love the food, thanking Connell for a delicious boar to fill their bellies with. At the end of the night, everyone followed Ainsley outside as she lit a torch for Sir Malcolm to see his way home. I watched from a small kitchen window, thinking how sad she must feel that her husband wasn't there with her. I wondered if he was in danger and if coming back was not safe for him. After everyone came inside I found my so-called bed and laid down, feeling all sorts of new aches from the day's work.

The work was honest and at times, rough, but I would miss the ladies of the castle. I barely had time to think about another thing before sleep captured me.

I woke at first light, strangely enough. I didn't have an alarm clock, but the cold room was so frosty that it served as one. I shivered in my dress and wished I could rip it off and put on a pair of sweatpants and a hoodie to stay warm. Oh how I longed for my comfy clothes.

I must have slept for about three hours, because I felt tired and groggy, but Ainsley allowed me leave, so I'd go. But first, I had to find a protector of sorts. That was going to be hard. I knew absolutely no one in this castle; no one I trusted anyhow. Trying to wake any of Sir Malcolm's men would prove difficult, because they were most likely still drunk from the night before. Scots really loved their whiskey.

Crawling up from my position on the floor, I once again snuck into the dressing room. I pulled off my dress and found just what I wanted, sort of. I couldn't find pants, so I settled for a buttery soft pair of stockings made from wool. I pulled on a brown and cream plaid skirt that was just a tad too large, which made me smile, and a white blouse. Over the blouse came a type of lace up bodice and then a thick wool shawl that matched the skirt. At least I was now warm and cozy and no longer looked like a maid. I had pulled out the satchel that held my glasses and clothing from when I first arrived here and planned to take that with me.

As I left the room, I found Iona in the kitchens preparing her meals. I had to say goodbye. If I found my bracelet I wasn't coming back here and she deserved some sort of explanation.

"Oh, lass, you gave me a fright. Where are you off to?" she asked, looking me over.

I took her hand in mine, "Iona, I want to thank you for all you've done to help me while I was here and even when we were at the castle before this. You've been real nice to me. I'll never forget that. I have to leave now. There's a mission I must attend to."

Her eyes went wide and then she nodded. "Tis okay, Mollie. I understand. But I wish you'd tell me where you're going."

I filled her in on as much as I could, without giving too much away about me not belonging here.

"Who will you take with ya?"

"I haven't the slightest clue, really. I was thinking Torren MacAllister, but I don't know him all that well."

Iona laughed, "Nae, Mollie. Do not ask any of that lot. They are not the sort you want taking you on an important trip like this one. No, you need someone who will protect ya. Times are hard right now and if, God forbid, you were to be attacked, you want someone strong." She bit her lip and drummed her fingers. "Ah! I've got it! You will be escorted by Eoin. He's the very best at tracking and he's a strong fighter, he is. Yes. I'll fetch him at once."

My face burned hot with embarrassment. I couldn't take Eoin. He was nice to me last night at the feast, smiling up at me as I served him, but who knew what kind of mood he'd be in today? Eoin's moods seemed to change with the weather.

Before I could protest, Iona was telling someone to wake him. My heart pounded as I waited in the kitchen for word on his refusal. When he came down the steps, I looked up to meet his gaze. He looked pissed. Yep, this was going to be horrible.

Bracing for his attitude, I remained quiet.

"So, I hear ye need a strong man to protect ye in the woods, eh?" he said as he grabbed a biscuit and chomped away at it, leaving crumbs all over his shirt. "Where are ye off to?"

His hair was a complete mess, and he looked like he rolled off a haystack just moments before.

"I... I need to ride two days to the nearest village to look for my bracelet. It's very important, and has great value," I told him. "Lady Ainsley advised me that I need someone to protect me. It wasn't my idea, by the way. I can do it myself—"

He chuckled. "Nae, ye can't. You aren't fit to ride

through these woods for two days, alone. That's foolish, and you know it. You'd be killed, raped, or worse without the proper escort."

He was right, and I knew that, but I didn't want to ride two days with someone who had anger issues. I truly knew nothing about this man, and he knew nothing about me.

"Well, let's get you fitted for a horse. I have just the one for you." I rolled my eyes. "Ye still have my thistle I see." He pointed to the flower that I had tucked between the fastenings of my shawl. I really wanted to preserve it somehow, for fear that it would wither up and die. It had dried nicely once I hung it upside down in the pantry, but throwing it out didn't seem right.

"It's pretty," I said, simply. Not giving him satisfaction of seeing the flower was my goal, but he laughed cockily. "I can find someone else to take me, I'm sure."

"Don't be daft, lass," Iona said coming between Eoin and me. "You know just as well that there are few in this castle who would take the time to help you on your quest. Just take the man and let him guide you."

She kissed my cheek and handed me a small leather pouch. "I've filled it with some dry goods and herbs. You'll find that most of the food will last ye, if you don't eat too much of it. This," she said handing me a leather canteen. "Will hold water for you both. Be careful out there, lass. And as soon as you can, come back to visit."

I don't know why or how, but I had a large sense inside telling me I wouldn't see her again. Reaching out I enveloped her into a hug. I didn't know her well, but she was the only one here I did know at all, really. She was always kind to me, even after I had been gone for so long. She had given me a job and a place to sleep. I would never forget that.

"Come now," Eoin said. "We must leave soon."

We walked to the stables to pick our horses, but on the way, Eoin said simply, "You never came to find me."

I looked up, completely confused, "What?"

"Last time we met, I told ye to come find me."

Oh yes, in the library. "I got busy." It was my only excuse.

"I see. No worry, then." Now I would wonder what he wanted from me, and I'd never know.

The horses neighed loudly as we entered the stables. The horsemaster was busily brushing a beautiful golden mare, who sniffed at me as I walked by.

"Eoin, what arc ye doing here so early, lad?"

"I'll need two horses, Graham. The lady and I are going to a village to search for a lost, what was it?"

Of course he'd forget what it was. "Family heirloom."

"Ah, an heirloom. Say, you haven't found anything here in the stables like that have ye? Or perhaps heard tell about anyone finding a rare." He paused, looking at me awaiting my answer.

"It's a bracelet. It goes around my wrist, and the color is rare, rose gold. It would be shiny in the sunlight." I remembered when I first received the bracelet, the feeling of immense sadness and joy at the same time. Sadness that Grandma had died, but joy that it was now my job to hold such power. Many people asked me about the bracelet and its importance; why I never took it off. My answer was usually simple, "It's important to me."

Truly, no one but Jessa understood its worth. If it were lost and I was in my time, I wouldn't be able to travel anymore. There was no replacement for the power the bracelet held. Every Librarian had a special item that allowed them to travel. Mine was that bracelet, and it was gone.

"I've not seen anything like that around here or heard tell of that. If I did happen to find it, I'd not say much to anyone, that's for sure. Hocking it for money would be the first thing I'd do."

That made me feel better about leaving the castle. It made me realize that someone perhaps did sell it and that this wasn't a wasted trip; that maybe there was some truth to what Ainsley said.

"I'll need two fine horses, man. Two not looking to keel over any day soon," Eoin said, not jokingly. He was serious, and for good reason. The horses weren't all in great shape.

"You know how hard it is to keep these horses, Eoin. I try me best." Poor Graham. He was nearly blind and I'm sure the cost to feed them was high. I wasn't even sure how the castle inhabitants were fed. The ins and outs of castle expenses really weren't my forte. Eoin patted Graham on the back and reassured him that once we were back, he'd help out more in the stables. Once he was done, he picked two horses. The golden mare and the strong black stallion that I wouldn't go near. He loaded them up with all that we'd need and then helped me up on my mare, whose name was Sloane. His horse he called Warrior. He did look like a warrior all right, just like Eoin himself. We rode down the hill and I turned Sloane around to take one last look at the castle. I'd never see this place again, and the feeling wasn't just that, it was a knowing. My heart told me it was so.

Ten

We rode until the sun came up fully into the sky and then we rode some more. We said all of two words to one another the whole time. Eoin mostly grunted at me to keep up, and I grunted back for him to shut up. The pain in my back and tailbone was worse with every passing hour. We only stopped for short intervals to feed and water the horses, allowing me to stretch and walk around. Finally, when the sun began to fade behind the trees, Eoin said it was time to stop for good. He tied the horses to a tree and we found a spot under thick foliage in which to start a small fire and bed down for the night. The cold began to seep into my very bones. I was dressed warmly, but not for the misty wet autumn night that we sat in. Eoin fed the fire and I pulled out the food Iona had packaged for us. Salted meat with what looked like a barley bread that was hard as a rock, was our dinner. I hadn't eaten meat since high school, but my stomach was near empty and I was starved. I was willing to chow down on the meat for the cause of being hungry. We ate in silence, chewing was exhausting and talking would do us in. I lay back onto the cold ground and rolled over away from Eoin. Sleeping in this confined space with a total stranger was weird, but the exhaustion prevented me from worrying too much about it.

I felt a blanket being tucked around me and drifted off to a light sleep hearing noises all night long. It was perhaps, the longest night of my life. Cracks from the fire, howls from animals, snapping twigs, it all kept me from a real, deep sleep. Eoin made no noise. No snoring, no grunting, and no movement. I found out in the morning, when the sun arose, that he had not been there. There was no Eoin next to me. The spot next to me was cold, as if no one had been there all night. I looked around and saw that I was completely alone. The fear of doing this by myself set in. He'd left me. He gave up and threw in the towel and went back to the castle. I was lost out here. I had no sense of direction and I was going to die.

Fumbling inside my satchel I found my glasses and put them on. At first they made me dizzy, since it'd been a while that I've been without them. But within a few minutes I was used to them again. Seeing things clearly would be important if I was alone. I ran my fingers through my tangled hair and felt like screaming out in frustration.

Standing up, I looked around for him, and noticed his horse was in fact gone.

"Coward!" I yelled to the empty forest. "Bastard, Eoin!"

I was royally screwed now. The cold morning showed my breath as I screamed aloud, venting my frustration. Yanking the blanket off the ground I wrapped it around my body hoping for warmth. The fire was still going so I sat down and tried to warm my cold hands. What was I going to do? I could go back and stay at the castle forever. At least

I'd have a home. Maybe I could settle down and have a few kids, raise them here in Scotland. I groaned at the thought.

Or I could venture to the town by myself. The threat of the English finding me and attacking me alone on the road was all too real. They were known to be horrible to women. So I guess I'd go back to the castle. Being a maid forever wasn't going to be my ideal life, but it sure beat death by the hands of the English.

"What the devil do ya have on yer face?"

I looked up startled. Eoin was there, carrying a dead rabbit carcass.

Standing fast I put my hands on my hips. He was getting my full attitude.

"I thought you left, you idiot! You scared the hell out of me. I thought I'd have to go back to the castle and be a maid forever."

He chuckled. "Is that so bad? Some say it's an honest job."

Rolling my eyes, I felt my glasses and pulled them off. He'd never seen glasses like mine before.

"These are spectacles, glasses, by the way. They help me see better."

He'd have to just get used to them, because I wasn't going to take them off again.

"Well, they are strange looking, but they look good on you. Can I see them?"

I nodded and handed them to him. He inspected them and put them on his face. "Och. They are horrid. I cannot see a thing. You say they help you see?"

"Yes. Now give 'em back to me."

"Sorry," he said, handing them back. "I didn't mean to scare ye. I went hunting early this morning. I had hoped for a stag but settled for a rabbit. Did ya sleep well enough?"

Shrugging I said, "Fine, I suppose if one doesn't mind all the sounds of nature. You didn't sleep at all, did you?"

"I did. I just didn't sleep next to you. I wanted you to be comfortable. It wasn't right for me to sleep so close to you. So, I slept by the horses. But that was far too cold, so I got up to hunt. Tonight though, I think I will sleep near you, if that's all right."

Surprised at his chivalry, I nodded. "You can. I have no problem. Actually, if we share body heat, we will stay warmer. We will sleep better if we're not freezing our butts off all night."

His eyes went wide and he sat down near the fire. "If you say so."

He began skinning the rabbit and handed me the fur. I took it, gagging slightly not sure what to do with it. Did he expect me to make him a pair of slippers with it? I set it aside and tried not to watch him clean the rest of the poor bunny.

"Do ye not like rabbit in your belly?"

I rolled my eyes. "I like food in my stomach, but I don't usually eat meat. I'm vegetarian."

The face he gave me was almost hilarious. I suppose Eoin was learning a lot by traveling with me.

"What in the world does that mean?"

"A vegetarian doesn't eat meat. They eat grains, beans, vegetables, and fruit. I do eat cheese, but I usually don't eat the cow that it comes from. It can be a healthier way of life, and for me, it was. I lost a lot of weight my senior... er ... when I was seventeen. I was a bit heavier than I am now."

He closed his mouth, and then nodded. Shoving a stick through the rabbit's mouth and out the hind end then placing it on the fire to cook.

"Looking at you, I'd say you should eat meat again,

you might blow away come the winter. Why do you think you needed to *lose weight* as you called it? Don't men in your village like a woman with meat on their bones? Do they prefer women who look like bones and skin?"

I laughed. If he'd only known what my life was like in high school. Boys, not men, would taunt me for being too fat. And after a while I got tired of not fitting into clothes the way I wanted. Shopping at plus sized clothing stores didn't exactly help me fit into high school life. If I wanted clothes for teens I couldn't find them there. I wore a lot of plaid and flowers. Finally, I lost the weight, the healthy way. I felt better for me, not for anyone else.

"No, the men in my village didn't really pay much attention to me. When you have red hair, glasses, and are big boned and heavier, they tend to ignore you. Not that I care very much for any of them."

He scoffed and looked away.

"Your hair is the first thing I noticed about you. It reminds me of the first sunset I ever saw. It burned up the sky and blazed across the ocean as far as the eye could see. My ma woke me up early just to see it. When I saw you, and your hair, it reminded me of that moment. The finest memory I have of her."

He looked at me, and we locked eyes. That was the most beautiful compliment I'd ever had about my hair, or anything really. Eoin was surprising me a lot. Maybe I had him pegged all wrong.

"That's why I was so rude to ya, when we first met. I don't like to think of my ma much. It hurts too bad. I should have been nicer to ya."

"It's fine," I said, as I picked grass to keep my hands busy. I found it hard to meet his eyes.

"Your shape, well any man who doesn't think you

beautiful needs to borrow your spectacles."

I blushed and looked away to hide my smile. The only compliments I'd received lately were on my skills as a student, not my looks. At the castle men mostly grunted for more ale and then said, "That'll do."

"Thanks. And, what am I supposed to do with this?" I asked holding up the rabbit fur. "Do you want me to make you a hat?"

He laughed.

"I'll keep it and trade it in the town. Put it inside yer bag for safe keeping, lass. This rabbit will be done in a bit. Are you hungry enough to eat this meat, or will you need some grass?" He asked nodding to my pile of grass I'd absentmindedly made.

"Oh, I think I'm hungry enough to eat two rabbits today."

After we ate, we set off once more. Eoin cleaned up the fire remnants, so the English wouldn't know we were there, just in case.

He said we didn't need to have them following our trail. Just like the day I arrived, a mist formed around the forest thickly. We rode through it using it to go unseen. I prayed we wouldn't encounter any soldiers but anything was possible now. Scotland wasn't what it is now, in my time. In my current situation I was living in the most horrific version of Scotland so far. And it would only get worse from here on out. The danger was real; it wasn't pretend. This was a time in which women were treated horribly by the English soldiers and the Scot's had no say in what was done to them or their families. I prayed that nothing like that would happen to us on this trip. If we made it to the town unscathed, I would be entirely grateful.

Eleven

The misty mountains held a sense of danger and beauty at the same time. Eoin would stop every so often and scout ahead of us to make sure there were no traps laid out awaiting our passage. If anything, Eoin was prepared and smart when it came to tracking and traveling. He was very protective.

This trip to Scotland had been incredibly different than the last times I had been here. I remembered the first trip here, I was terrified. I knew that the English were not going to go easy on any of Sir Malcolm's followers and being with him made me a target. When I had landed safely back at home, I was more than pleased. Jessa wasn't sure why I was kissing the ground, but once I explained to her the danger I had just been in, she was in agreement that this was one of my most dangerous missions. It wasn't anything like the trip to Paris in 1982, to study a famous French artist in her prime. She was fantastic and so was her art. Everything about Paris was lovely. As we rode our horses, I dreamed I was there instead of the cold drizzly Scotland I was in now.

"Are you deep in thought?" Eoin asked, breaking my illusion.

I nodded. "I was thinking about another place and another time." He rode a little ahead of me and held up his hand, shushing me quickly.

His eyes darted around wildly searching the woods. My skin crawled with fear as he signaled me to stay quiet and stay put. I hated being told what to do, but in this case, being protected by Eoin was the main point. I steadied Sloane and patted her damp hair. Warrior neighed quietly and Eoin pulled back his reigns quickly to quiet him. He eased ahead and I did as he said. Once he was out of sight, I had a feeling I didn't like very much and it wasn't fear, it was the lack of protection.

Twelve

Being a Librarian prepared me for time-traveling through ancient times, searching relics, and artifacts, but it did not prepare me for self-defense in the Middle Ages. I wasn't accustomed to having to fight for my life. I wasn't even armed with a weapon of any sort. With Eoin gone, I was defenseless. Remaining on Sloane was my best bet since I could ride away in hopes of getting away from danger. Granted I didn't know where the castle was now that we were so far into the woods. I had no idea where we were at all really.

I heard shouting ahead and my arms tensed, prepared to take Sloane into the hills above me to hide out. When Eoin crashed through the woods, his face was calm and this in turn calmed me.

"Sorry, Mollie," he said breathlessly. "I've encountered a weary traveler but nothing more than that. He did give me the safest route to the village, lucky enough. Glad I found him when I did."

I hated that Eoin and I were now becoming friends because he didn't really know me at all. He thought my name was Mollie from Aberdeenshire. He had told me so much about his mother already and here I was being a liar. Doing what I was best at.

I shook off the deceit and followed him into the wild woods. His long blond hair was once again pulled back into a low ponytail and wrapped in leather. He looked amazing with long hair. I wondered why he didn't let it flow around him all wild and free. I looked at his back and wondered what he looked like with regular clothes on instead of a leather overcoat and kilt. He'd fit in so well in 2018, much better than I even did.

"My ma loved the woods," he said, breaking my trance. "Did your ma like to take walks in the woods?"

I shook my head. "My mother is complicated as a mother and a person," I began. "She and I no longer speak."

He turned his head around to look at me when I said that.

"How could ya not speak to your ma? I couldna go a day without speaking to mine. Sure, she'd make me mad as a hornet, but I eventually came round."

Complicated wasn't going to cut it anymore. He'd need some more details than that now.

"I was given a gift when I was young, and with it a big responsibility. It was handed down from my grandma, and this made my mother very envious of me. She didn't understand why I was given the gift and not her, but that was just the way my grandma did it. The way my family did it for centuries. So, she took on the responsibility of teaching me, and as each year passed, her jealousy and rage became worse. When my father left us, that made it much harder. She took everything out on me, her anger and her pain. So I chose to leave and not look back."

Eoin pulled his reigns, slowing his horse down to

match Sloane's stride. He nodded and listened to me talk, never once saying a word about my choice.

"My father and I are bullheaded and we fought more than we did anything else," he said, looking out into the distance. "I hated when he had to leave my ma to go to his wife in marriage. I know he loved my ma, it was there in their eyes. He always told me it was a sin to love two women and that his punishment was that he had to split his heart into two pieces; one for his wife and one for my ma. But once I challenged him and asked if he could only split it into two pieces, where did his love for me go?"

I swallowed hard, feeling the pain emanate from Eoin in the very air around us. He was damaged, like me.

"His answer was, 'That's another punishment that I must bear. That I have no love left for my only son.' It crushed me then. But now, now, it doesn't hurt much anymore. He died after my ma did. He had caught what she had and I cared for him while he lay on his sickbed. I was the only one to do it. I did not want to. Is that a sin in God's eyes?"

I shook my head.

"No, absolutely not. I think fathers should love their children, no matter what. But that's the thing about free will. I think my father has forgotten I existed, because it's been years since I've heard from him. He's living in France with his other family. I mean, how could he even think about me after all these years? I'm forgettable."

Eoin's hand reached out and touched my arm, gently. This small act sent chills up my arm and down my body. His hands were rough but soft at the same time. I didn't want him to remove them.

"Don't do that."

"What?" I asked, my eyes welling up with damned

tears again.

"Make yerself sound like something that has no worth. I cannot bear to hear it again. You need to see yerself like I see you. You are anything but forgettable."

I shook my head and laughed.

"I can only imagine what you see." My heated cheeks burned once again. Eoin had made me do a lot of blushing on this trip and he'd also made me feel a strange sensation when he touched me.

"Follow me," he said, taking his horse off into a full run. I kicked Sloane and we flew through the trees and around streams. We headed up, up, up, into the woods gaining climate so fast that I was scared to look down. Finally, we came out into an open field at the top of the hill we were just screaming through.

Eoin slowed Warrior, and Sloane followed suit. I pulled my shawl up over my shoulders as the air up here was much colder.

"You see the sun in the sky?" Eoin asked pointing to the burning sun above our heads. "You see how it touches all that it can? Spreading all over the land."

I nodded, taking notice that the view from here was absolutely breathtaking.

"Yeah, it's so gorgeous out here. I could look at this view every day."

He nodded in agreement, and said, "That's what you are like." He turned away from the view and looked directly at me. "You look much like that sun. You touch everything you pass. You rise up and burn bright, for me, and for all the men at the castle. They do not keep quiet when a bonnie lass comes to visit. I had to get you out of their sights for a while, for fear that they'd scoop you up and take you from me."

My breath caught and my heart beat faster. I had never, ever, been told anything so flattering before Eoin. He was a rare human. And it was then that I realized I had been very, *very* wrong about the kind of person he was. He showed me that you cannot judge someone from a first impression. I had thought that Trevor was a good person, with his dashing smile and his cheery talk. That's all he was; talk. But Eoin, he was different. He was at first, I'll admit, a bit hard to take in, but now, he'd proven that he could be trusted and that he had my best interests at heart.

"I am not a good person, Mollie. I am bad. In my soul, you see, it's damaged. My father, he did something to me by not loving me, and it ruined me. But when you came, you awakened something inside of me. I can feel things, like I did when Ma was alive. I want to help you get your bracelet back, but I do not want you to leave the castle. I need your brightness to help me be happy again."

It was me this time who reached out to touch him. Instinct drew me to him as I ran my fingers over his and gently pulled away, before it was too much for him.

"I have to tell you something," I said, quietly. It was time to get as honest with him as he had been with me. That was only fair. "My name isn't really Mollie."

My accent fell away and I was being me; the real me.

Thirteen

Eoin's eyes grew wide as his hands gripped the reigns. He looked upon me bewildered, but he graciously let me have my say.

"My real name is Savannah, and I am not from Scotland, as I'm sure you've now guessed." I waited a moment, giving it time to settle. He shook his head but then said, "Go on, then, explain, lass."

"I'm from a small town, called Brewster in a state called North Carolina. I know much of this won't make any sense to you, but I can't lie to you anymore. I mean, lying is part of my job, but I don't like it one bit. You remember that gift that was given to me by my grandma?"

He nodded but said nothing.

"It was the gift to travel through time. So, where I come from the year is 2018. My job was to come here, to Scotland, and find Sir Malcolm Walsh. You see, in my time he's hailed as a hero, but there is little knowledge about where he resided when he went into hiding. We know how he died, but not where he was the whole time. And my job was to get that information, to fill in the holes. I know it sounds impossible and the fact of time-travel is bewildering, but I'm being honest with you." Telling Eoin the truth laid me bare. I stood the chance to become thrown into shackles and strung up as a witch. But I saw something in Eoin, something that said he would trust and believe me.

For a few moments he worried his lip and looked anywhere but my eyes. Finally he laughed and asked me, "So you know when he died do ya? Then why on earth are ya still here then, lass?"

I shook my head, confused, because I just explained that. Perhaps he was testing me and trying to see if what I said was the truth. Catching me in a lie would show I was a liar.

"To find out where he is hiding. I told you that."

"Yeah, but you just said... wait you don't know exactly when he dies, do ya?"

"Yes, I do know that. He will be caught in 1304 and hang for his crimes against the English crown. I just didn't want to tell you that, is all. I know that you are with his men and that you're rallying around him."

Eoin laughed his hearty laugh and jumped down from his horse. Angry now that I was being laughed at, I got down from mine. He was being an ass again. I guess his moods changed much like the Scottish weather, because the sun went away and grey clouds began to form.

"What is so funny about this? You don't believe me?"

It wasn't normal for a traveler to tell their targets or the people surrounding them who they really were. I was going way against the rules, but I had lost my bracelet and that was cardinal rule number one, and I screwed that up. So I figured, what the heck!

"It's not that I don't believe ya, lass. Granted, your story is a bit odd, but we can come back to that. What is so funny is that in your future they've got it all wrong. Sir Malcolm Walsh is dead already. Very dead. So how can he die in six years, *again?* Will they bring him back to life then, and then re-kill him?" He chuckled and then kicked up a spot of grass with his toe. He seemed tense and angry. Perhaps it was because he thought me crazy.

No! He couldn't be dead. Eoin must be wrong.

"You don't know what you're talking about, Eoin," I said. "I know what the future holds for him, and we are *not* wrong. Historians have studied this man for centuries."

"Ye are wrong, woman! I can prove it to ya."

I shook my head. Maybe they told the castle's inhabitants that he was dead, but they were all so mistaken. Perhaps they wanted to keep it hushed and only a few people knew he still lived. Maybe, there was a traitor in the castle, ready to out his whereabouts the minute they found out the truth. I wasn't sure, but when they caught him in six years, it would shock a lot of people. They did think him dead when he was in hiding. Sure, that's what Eoin thought. But what of his proof?

"Get on with this so-called proof, then," I challenged.

He began taking off his coat, and the breeze blew harder, tossing his hair free from the tie. *What on earth was he doing?* When the coat came off, he began taking off his white blouse.

"Eoin, please put your clothes back on," I urged. "You are proving nothing except that you're getting naked."

When the shirt was removed, Eoin displayed another piece of fabric, this time it was a clan tartan that should have been worn on the outside over the jacket. Instead, he was wearing it underneath his clothing, as if hiding it.

I still didn't understand how this proved that Malcolm was dead.

"Do you know this clan tartan?" he asked, boldly.

Looking at the colors I knew I had seen it before, but I wasn't sure where. The blue and the brown with hints of green had been colors that I had indeed seen before.

Then it hit me, it was the tartan of Clan Walsh.

"Why are you wearing that?" I asked.

"Because, Sir Malcolm Walsh, *the hero*, was my father. I was there when he took his last breath. You see, your future is wrong. He doesn't get caught for his crimes against the crown in six years, because I was the one to bury him. Just like I was the one who rode all the way from my home to the hidden castle where his wife lived. He made me promise to tell her and only her of his death. I had to go there, to be at her side and help her, if need be. It was an oath he made me swear to uphold. I'm there, day after day, lying to his many supporters giving them a false hope.

"I'm his bastard son, you can imagine just how welcomed I was to the one wife who couldn't have any of his children. She was less than happy to see me. When I told her he was dead, she fainted."

My mouth fell open. I had no words for this confession; only shock. The man I had traveled through time, and gotten stuck here for, was dead. My whole universe was literally in ruins. I felt like fainting, too. Instead, I sat down on the ground and the rain began.

"Lass, are you okay?"

He was asking *me* if I was okay? He just confessed that he was the bastard son of the man so many hailed as a hero, had heard I was from the future, and had no family left. Eoin was totally and completely alone here. I wondered if he still thought I was like the sun.

"I'm stuck here, Eoin."

He shook his head.

"No. I will help you up, stubborn lass."

I pushed his hands away. "No. The bracelet that's missing. Without it, I am stuck here in Scotland, in this time. I can't go back home. Ever."

"Is it magic?"

"Sort of."

"Well, hmm." He began biting his lip again.

Yeah, that about summed it up. We were quite the pair.

"What if we find it, can you go home?" he asked, running his hands over his chin.

I nodded. Then realized not once did Eoin question my story. He didn't run for the hills or accuse me of lying, like I basically did him.

"Do you believe me?" I asked, hopeful.

He sat down across from me and shrugged his shoulders. "Whether I believe your story doesn't really matter. What matters is that you do. You know there is talk of fairies, maybe you are one. You do fit the description."

I laughed. "Aren't they small?"

"Oh no, they can yield magic. You could have made yourself grow into a full size human-like woman. You do have that way of overcoming me with yer beauty."

I laughed, not knowing if he was serious or not. "You have to be joking. You actually believe that?"

He shrugged his shoulders. If that's what helped him believe me, who was I to dispel that notion? I decided to get up and get back onto the horse. We rode in the rain until finally Eoin saw how drenched I was. There was an abandoned, at least I thought it was, cottage hidden amongst the trees. If Eoin hadn't seen it I never would have.

He jumped from his horse making a loud splash in a puddle and pulled my mare along with him.

"We'll stay here tonight. But we must go before first light."

Nodding, I got down and followed him into the home. The thatched roof had need of repair, but it was better than sleeping in the rain. Eoin cleaned out the fireplace and I cleaned a spot on the ground for us to sleep. I had slept in some pretty rough places, but nothing as bad as this. The spiders were making this house their haven and I hated spiders.

"It's pretty dirty," I said, realizing that I was still speaking without an accent. It was nice to finally be myself. Continually speaking in another language can be exhausting after a while.

"Oh, Mollie, er, I mean... what's yer real name again?"

I laughed. "It's Savannah. But try not to call me that in front of people. It's not a common name and it will be strange. Also, when we make it to town, I'll be pretending I'm Scottish, again. If that's okay with you? I'd rather not be arrested for witchcraft or—"

"Pretending yer Scottish?"

"Yeah, that."

He laughed as he got a small fire started in the empty fireplace.

"It must be strange to keep up such a rouse. How do you go about that?"

It *was* strange. I explained how I had Jessa make the dress that I wore the first day I arrived, and how I studied Gaelic to prepare for the journey. Along with all the months of preparation that came with it. Then I told him the odd circumstances that brought me back; how the book had called to me.

"I've been here before. I met your father. He was very nice to me," I told him. He only rolled his eyes. "He's nice to all the lassies. Try having him as your father."

I realized that because I had met him a few times and read false stories about him, Sir Malcolm was proving to not be the man I thought he was. Everything I was learning here was being recorded in his book. Which meant his history would change and he wouldn't be the man so revered. Just then, it hit me.

"Oh my God!"

Eoin grabbed his knife and jumped up. "What is it?"

I laughed but tried to bury it down.

"Nothing. I just realized something is all."

I couldn't believe I hadn't thought of it before now. If everything was being reported as I went along, then Jessa knew where I was. She could send a Librarian inside the book to help me out. All she'd have to do was visit the Historical Society of Libraries and tell them I was stuck.

Unless two things: She didn't look inside the book for me or she thought I ran away for a few days to think. Maybe she wasn't even worried about me. It wasn't unlike me to go off for a few days without telling her. But, I would eventually text her to tell her I was all right. I could only hope that she would notice my absence and realize it wasn't me trying to get away.

Fourteen

"**D**o you have the food?**"** Eoin asked, changing the subject entirely. When his belly growled, I understood why.

I nodded and pulled out the satchel. The food was tucked neatly inside, but as I dug for it, I found that it was soaked and ruined.

"Crap!" I tried to dig around to see if any of the food was salvageable, but to no avail. The meat was soggy and the bread mush.

"Well, I suppose I need to go for a hunt," Eoin exclaimed, standing up.

"I thought that it would stay safe inside this," I told him. "I'm sorry."

"Nay, lass. Do not apologize to me for something that the rain did. You are not at fault. I crave a hunt. I will find something for us to eat. Worry not."

He grabbed his own satchel and pulled a bow and quiver of arrows free. Thinking maybe I could help I stood up and felt the world beneath me rock side-to-side.

"Whoa, lass. Steady yourself."

Eoin helped me back down gently and I took the hand offered. He laid my head back and put a hand to my head.

"You feel feverish," he said, upon inspection. "When was the last you ate?"

"This morning, before we left the last camp. But I felt fine before this. I wasn't really hungry." Now though, my stomach churned in anger craving food and I felt nauseous at the same time. The feeling was odd and unlike anything I'd felt before. Maybe I'd caught some rare stomach bug from someone in the castle and was now feeling the effects of it. I wasn't even sure if that was possible or not.

"I'll get you something to eat. Stay here and rest a while." I nodded and let myself recover from whatever had happened to me. As I closed my eyes, I thought about home and all that I had left behind. The nights here were the worst. They made me crave what I was missing and brought back all the memories of what I left behind. The fight with my mother played over and over in my head. Leaving the way I had left so many things up in the air. Jessa was smart, no doubt she was looking for me and as my protector was doing all she could to find a way to get me back.

I looked out the small hole that used to be a window in this broken down cottage and watched the rain fall upon the greenery outside. Scotland was in a way becoming my home. The very thought of living here forever was horrible, no doubt due to the time I was in, but as a country, it would be amazing.

Eoin, well he was unpredictable and surprised me in many ways. At first, I had thought him very a different person. He was truly growing on me. He was much like me, he had a rough upbringing that forced him to grow up faster than he wanted, I'm sure. With his father being the man he was, Eoin was fatherless, like me. Sure, he had been rough to me when we first met, now I knew the reasons behind all of that tough exterior. I, in many ways, was much like him. I wasn't the cheeriest person to be around. I held onto a lot of my anger from my upbringing and tended to take it out on the people around me.

At school I distanced myself from everyone because I wasn't happy with my life. And I could see that in Eoin. He pushed me away, and probably everyone else, because he was unhappy.

I waited for what seemed like hours for Eoin to come back. And even drifted off to sleep. Finally, I felt his presence and woke up to him cooking over the fire.

"Tis almost done, lass. You should wake up and eat something." He handed me a slice of meat. Without question I ate it up and almost licked my fingers to savor the flavor.

"I caught three of them," Eoin said, as he handed me more. "Just... keep eating and try not to look at what it is I killed."

Smiling, I did as he said. He didn't want me to see what it was, because of my sensitivity I'm sure. What he didn't know was that I didn't care what I was eating at the moment. I was just happy to have a full belly. My sick feeling started to go away a bit, but not completely. I needed to rest and get this mission completed so I could get home.

"It's delicious, Eoin. Thank you, really," I said, as I sat back. "My stomach thanks you."

He nodded and cleaned up the mess he'd made and ate the leftovers. I laid back watching him as he did.

"What is it about this bracelet that can get you home exactly?" he asked, sitting down and wrapping himself in his large wool blanket. I looked down at his bare legs and his kilt and wondered if he ever got a chill from weather like this wearing that.

"If ye want to see my kilt, come have a closer look then," he said, pointing to it.

My cheeks went red. "What?"

He had caught me staring openly at his crotch. I was embarrassed beyond belief. The words didn't come fast enough for me to reply. I just looked away.

"You were looking at it. Come take a closer look at the colors. They're beautiful are they not?"

Oh! Thank goodness. He thought I was looking at the colors in his tartan kilt and not, well anything indecent.

Many men of this era wore their family's colors, but I knew his family's colors were underneath him, hiding.

I slid closer taking in the differences in color. I liked this tartan better than his father's colors. These colors were brighter greens and blues.

"Whose colors are these if they're not your father's?" I asked.

"My ma's. This kilt belonged to her brother, my uncle. He died in the war, bravely. I wear it proudly."

I decided not to tell him that I liked it better. I lay back again, watching him tend to the fire.

"Funny thing fire," he said, as he played with it. "I burnt my father and mother in a pyre when they died. I couldn't tell anyone that my father died. That's not easy to hide, you know."

I nodded, understanding full well what hiding things was like.

"Lying isn't easy."

"Tell me about the bracelet, now. What does it look like?"

I described it in full detail, so that when we went into the town, he would know exactly what he was searching for.

"How does it work?"

I sighed, not knowing how to explain this part.

"Well, traveling through time was all part of a scientist, Harold Lockhart's plan. He wrote a formula, a sort of spell if you like, that allows only certain people from a particular family, to travel through time. We record history. It's our job to record it correctly so that historians can teach those in future generations. Often times it's the historians who make mistakes when they're learning about a famous figure, so we go back in time to double check. Lockhart's a genius for coming up with the Librarians. It's the perfect way to hide time travelers."

"What are librarians?"

I laughed. If anyone in my time had asked me that, I'd smack them.

"They have the best job. They work with books. Their job is very important. Some librarians even help people learn to love books. I want to be an archivist someday and work in the historical library archives, but that's beside the point.

I believe you have librarians in this time period, but you refer to them as monks. They copy the words from one book to another. And to be exact, the first library in France will emerge in the next century. You'll someday hear about libraries and those that care for the books there, and you can think of me."

He smiled at me and said, "I could never forget you, lass. I'll think of you every time I see this." He pointed to my thistle. "My *cluaran*." *Cluaran* meant thistle in Gaelic.

Eoin was definitely a charming Scot, proving to me again and again that I judged him too harshly upon our first meeting. I silently wished that he could have been around in my time. A guy like him would change my whole outlook on life.

Continuing on I explained the way we traveled and how the bracelet protected me and kept me from being stuck in that time, like I was now. He didn't say a word; just listened intently.

"When I came this time, it was different," I told him. "I had a horrible night, the night before. So I got up early and went to the library. I wanted to read, but I saw him—"

"Saw who?" His eyes grew wide in wonder.

"The boy responsible for my horrible night. I ran downstairs, trying to avoid him, planning to read in my office. And that's when I heard music coming from the book. I picked it up and was sucked inside." I clapped my hands for effect and Eoin jumped, then laughed. "Now I sit. Stuck. Without the bracelet I cannot go back."

Eoin shrugged. "You could have been stuck somewhere worse. There is no place more bonnie than Scotland, lass. Maybe the book wanted you to come here. It's like... that fairytale from when I was a lad."

I looked up, curious. "What fairytale?"

"There's a beautiful lady, who is called to Scotland from a faraway land. She's lost, in her life, you see. She's not happy in the castle that she lives in and she is called to the woods of Scotland by the bagpipes." Just then chills crawled along my body because that's exactly what my story is.

I am the girl in the castle, unhappy and lost. I couldn't help it as tears fell down my face.

"Don't ya cry lass, are you ill again?"

"No," I said, "I just... I am the girl in that story." The tears kept falling as Eoin reached across, slowly, and wiped them away with his surprisingly soft hands. I hadn't been this close to him before now, but I don't dislike it. His eyes held concern as he wiped my tears away and I knew that he wanted to make me feel better.

"Savannah, do ye think you really are the girl in the story? Were ye lost?"

I nodded, vehemently, unable to talk.

"I was lost, myself."

He put his hands on my shoulders pulling me into a hug that I didn't know I needed. But I didn't move or pull away. Instead I fell asleep in the warm embrace of a man that I hardly knew but trusted with my life.

****

"Savannah, time to wake lass," Eoin said, shaking me gently. "There ye are. I can't let you sleep all day. We are close to the town."

I nodded and rubbed the sleep from my eyes. I sat up and yawned, then realized, I needed to brush my teeth in the worst way. What did the Scots use for toothbrushes in the woods?

I stood up and excused myself to use the bathroom and found a cozy little corner to relieve myself. Afterwards I found a bristle-like leaf that I rubbed along my teeth and tongue to clean what I could. I could use a hairbrush, but that was pushing it. Instead I pulled it back into another braid and tucked the pieces in, keeping it out of my face. I was feeling better today but I wasn't as clear minded as I wanted to be.

"I need a shower," I told Eoin. "You know where I come from we bathe daily. We also call it a shower. We stand up and the water comes out of pipes to wash us." His eyes grew wide, as he handed me the reigns to my mare.

"Daily?"

I nodded. "We also brush our teeth and hair several times a day. But here, things are much dirtier."

He laughed. "I take care of my teeth, but I don't bathe daily. Maybe when the sun warms the lake you'll find me there, but I don't need a bath now. I smell dandy."

I shivered. "You should really do it more often, a lot of people in this time die from disease. That can occur when you're not clean and don't take good care of yourself."

He laughed. "Concerned for me are ye?"

I huffed and looked away.

We rode along the path, keeping off the main roads. And soon I heard the sounds of other people coming from up ahead. We finally made it to the village.

I was elated. It was perhaps the longest, strangest trip I'd ever had. But having Eoin along made it a whole lot easier. If I hadn't listened to Iona I don't know if I would have made it to the village.

Small children played games, chasing after one another, as their parents no doubt worked hard to tend their farms and houses. The older children worked alongside them.

I didn't see where anyone would have gone to trade anything like jewels, but I trusted that Eoin knew where to go.

He led our horses into the village as people eyed us as we passed by. Eoin got off his horse and walked up to a man who was taking care of a stable of horses. These horses were well fed, and I realized that he knew what he was doing. I jumped off of the horse and led her to the water to drink. She gulped it down happily. Tucking my glasses into my bag, I let Eoin do all the talking.

"We need to find a tradesman, if you have one," he

asked in Gaelic. The man nodded and pointed toward what looked like a pub. "Thank you."

We walked on and ignored the stares that came from everyone we passed. I wondered if they hadn't seen people in a while. This made me nervous. What if my bracelet wasn't here? What would I do then? That was something I didn't consider. If it wasn't here, what was plan B? Did I have a plan B?

Eoin led me to the pub and asked me to stay outside.

"Oh, no. I will handle my own business, and I'm not afraid to go inside there," I said, pointing to the door.

"It's no place for a lass like you, Savannah," he whispered. "Taverns can be rough and the men are not to be trusted. I don't want to have to knock a man in the head if I don't have to."

I sighed. "What do you plan to trade for it, if it's in there?" I asked.

He pulled free a bag of coins. I shook my head. "I have something they might want more. If its someone not wanting to part with it for coin they might like this," I said producing my cell phone. I had found it in my pocket the day I left the castle. I had tucked my clothes inside the bag I took with me and noticed my useless cell sticking out of my pants pocket. I hadn't thought it important then, but now, it was something interesting to someone in the middle ages. Eoin's face was the proof.

"What the devil is that?"

I laughed and turned it on. "This is a cell phone, but more about that later. To someone in there, it's magic. Let's go."

He growled and followed me inside.

Fifteen

The smell hit me like a brick to the face. A brick that smelled like dirty rotten drunk cheese. I gagged, fighting the urge to run right back out the door. Men were sitting down drinking away all their woes, while the ladies sat on their laps and whispered sweet tales in their ear.

I guess they didn't care that it was still morning, it was five o'clock somewhere, maybe even back home. Eoin pulled my arm and took the lead. I decided to let him do the talking, since he seemed to know how a tavern operated. I, in fact did not. That wasn't something I studied.

"Is there a tradesman here?" he asked a man leaning against a pole.

The man said nothing, just pointed to a dark corner in the back. Of course it was the darkest place in the whole tavern, because why wouldn't it be? Why would someone honest be in a place like this?

Following Eoin, I tried not to listen to the catcalls from the drunks around me. It was not hard to, when they all thought I was a lady of the night, or heck, a lady of the day in this case. I rolled my eyes and bit my tongue. I wanted nothing more than to go up and slap them.

Eoin led us to the dark corner where a woman sat, drinking ale from a large pewter cup.

"Help ya?" she asked, licking the froth from her lips. She wasn't pretty, but you could tell that her looks mattered to her nonetheless. She had her hair neatly styled, and even put some sort of blush on her cheeks. Her lips were bright red and as she smiled so were her teeth. Whatever she was using to stain her lips had certainly rubbed off, either that or she had just eaten the last person who traded with her. I cringed at the thought.

"We're looking for a specific item," Eoin began, as he sat down across from her. I took a seat as well, trying to look brave.

"Aye, and what would that be then?"

"My lady here, needs a prize for her arm. And I mean to buy her one. A bracelet to be exact. It needs to be as bonnie as her," he said, smiling and leaning closer to the woman. "Do ye have an item like that?"

I worried that she would have kept it for herself, or perhaps she didn't even have it. Her face was stern as she sat back in her seat. She kept very still, saying nothing for several agonizing minutes.

"What's yer name, lad? I like to know who I am sitting with ya see," she purred, flashing those red teeth.

"Eoin."

"Eoin, what a fine name. I'm Marleighn," she said. "And you?"

"Mollie," I said simply, using my fake accent.

"Bah, not a fancy name at all! A lady with a fine name deserved jewels. And yer man here, he wishes to purchase you jewels does he not?"

I wasn't sure how it was any of her business, but for the sake of playing the part, I wrapped my hands around his arm and nodded.

"Aye, that he does but I cannot help the name my ma gave me. Do you have a bracelet Marleighn?"

She shook her head. "Nay, but I have a ring. I don't see that you have one of those."

My heart fell and I felt as if I had been punched in the stomach. If she didn't have the bracelet then I wasn't sure what to do next. What was my next plan of attack?

"Now, Marleighn, I am hoping we can make a friendly trade here. I know ye have bracelets," Eoin said. "I've been told you are the one to see. My friend, he wouldn't do me wrong."

Well, perhaps trusting Eoin to do the talking and planning was my best bet. I could see that she wasn't going to care for the fur that Eoin had given me, Marleighn would want something special.

She laughed. "Who's yer friend? The man that sold it to me?"

I looked up. So she did have it!

"Yes. Good lad he is," Eoin said, playing the part well. "He and I go back for many years. He was at our wedding."

Marleighn smiled, truly looking happy to hear that we were married as Eoin fed her lies. She happily gulped them down.

"He was a nice man," she said, agreeing. "He always finds the best items that Finn does!"

"Finn!" I exclaimed. He stole my bracelet? What a dirty rotten jerk. I knew that I couldn't trust him and that something was off about him the day I first landed in that bloody field. Sure, he'd given me a ride to the castle, but he had been rude and stern shortly after.

"He said he found it on a lass drunk, face down in a horse stall," Marleighn laughed. "Told me she was just begging to have it stolen from her arm. He slipped it off and she didn't notice."

I forced myself to laugh along with Eoin, but in reality, I wanted to strangle Marleighn then find Finn and do the same. Instead of helping me that night, he ripped my bracelet off of my arm and sold it to this bitch. I growled inside, the fire of anger burning hotly.

"I'll trade ye for it," she said, getting down to business. "But I want something just as fine as it is." She reached down into a box and pulled my bracelet out. It was right there in front of me yet I couldn't touch it.

"What is a fine lady like yourself looking for?" Eoin asked, patting my leg under the table. I'm sure the anger rolled off of me in waves. "Coin? Gold?"

Marleighn shook her head and smiled like a creepy Cheshire cat.

"I may have something yer looking for, my good lady," Eoin said, leaning close. "It's not something any of the folk around here have ever seen before. And it's... well, it's magic."

Marleighn's eyes bugged out of her head in interest. She almost began drooling. "What is it?"

I pulled the cell phone out of my bag and laid it gently on the table. The glittery black case sparkled near the dancing candle flame.

"Tis magic of the Fae," I began in my storyteller type voice. The time for getting my bracelet back was now. No more joking around.

"The good fair folk have made these for only the special Fae who have worked so hard. These boxes make pictures come alive in rich color. Would you like to see?"

She nodded eagerly. I turned it on, and instantly it started dinging loudly as it booted up. There wasn't anything I could do about that now but let my cell do its job. Marleighn scooted closer watching my cell bring up the home screen. A picture of me and Jessa came up and Marleighn eyed me.

"That's you!"

I nodded. "Yes, it is."

"Oh, what a rare and special box. May I touch it?"

Quickly I took it away before she did. "Oh no. Not until we get that fine bracelet," I said. Then, thinking about Eoin I said. "Along with coin."

She nodded and pulled free a large coin purse, dropping it on the table. "I'll give all that I can now. And the bracelet. What else does it do?"

I played a short song from my downloaded music and she bobbed her head to it. I had her hook line and sinker and Eoin knew it. He turned to me and smiled.

"You sure you're okay with parting with it?" he asked as she played with the magic box.

I nodded. "All of that stuff is stored in my cloud."

He shook his head and laughed. "I've no clue what that means. But if you're okay, then so am I."

I took the bracelet from a very happy and dazed Marleighn and gave Eoin the bag of money and we hightailed it out of there as fast as we could.

We rode as far as our horses would take us, neither of us saying where we thought to go next, just riding. The sun on my face and the Scottish wind in my hair made me happier than I had been since I arrived. As we reached a glen, I realized I hadn't put the bracelet back on yet, and I knew why.

I was afraid of leaving Eoin just yet. Watching him as

he pet his monster horse, I felt an ache inside that I'd never felt before during a trip. I'd never not wanted to go home. All I wanted for the past week was to go home and now I wanted to stay.

Suddenly Eoin's head jerked up and he said, "English! Ride fast, Savannah!"

I looked back to see that he was right, there were two Englishmen riding our way. That spelled trouble. If the English caught me and Eoin out here in the open there was no telling the savagery that could take place.

I kicked Sloane, urging her to run, and run she did. She ran alongside Eoin and his horse as we crested the top of the hill, but we weren't safe yet. The English were close to us still. Stopping here, out in the open wasn't an option. Eoin jumped down from Warrior and pulled him alongside a small stream.

"I hope you have a plan, you crazy Scot! Walking through this stream is slowing us down!"

"Aye, I do. Now hush and follow me." We now walked through the stream, and my feet began to freeze over as the cold water rushed over them. I was not dressed for Scotland's wetland. As a matter of fact, no one in Scotland was well dressed for this place. The shoes were barely shoes, the clothes were thin, and then there was his kilt, we could just keep going on and on about that thing.

I didn't see the waterfall at first but I heard it. Putting two and two together, I knew we were heading toward it to either jump over it or hide in it. I hoped it was the latter.

I was thankful when Eoin led us around it as we finally came upon it. The water was rushing very fast now and I was surprised at how the little stream had come from such a magnificent waterfall. The mist touched me as we walked our horses behind the rushing water into a rather large cave.

"I used to hide here and watch my father return to Ainsley," he admitted. "He never found me here. But I suspect he knew he had someone watching him."

"How far away are we from the castle?" I asked as I wrapped my arms around myself.

"Not far, now. Just need to keep away from trouble."

I agreed and shivered. "Lass, come closer, I'll keep ya warm. And I promise to be a gentleman."

He opened his arms and I leaned in. The hugs this man gave could warm your very soul. His mere body was like a heater in this wet climate. I was thankful he had so much warmth at that moment.

As he held me, he watched out of the stream of water for the English patrol. The water was rushing so fast I don't know how he could see, but he did.

He leaned against the rocky cave and pulled me with him. I nestled in and let myself stay warm. Then the shivering stopped and he let me go. Instantly I wanted to be back in his arms again.

"They're gone," he said, pulling on Warrior.

"Oh. Okay, then. I suppose you should get back to the castle."

He turned, giving me a strange look. "You mean we should go, no?"

I didn't like this part. I actually dreaded having to do this once I got the bracelet, but it was inevitable.

"It's time for me to go home, Eoin. You can go back to the castle and perhaps you'll tell the truth to the others about your dad, or maybe you'll keep the secret. I don't know. But I've done my job. I've found out what happened to Sir Malcolm Walsh and, as an added bonus, I met his son. I won't forget you or the small adventure we've had. But my home is calling to me."

He shook his head and his face looked sad and angry. "Are you certain you've done all that you meant to do? There may be more you have to learn about him. I have lots of stories."

I smiled. "You may be right, but I figured out why I have been feeling so ill lately. It's time sickness. It can happen when you spend too much time traveling. My body isn't meant for this era, and I am feeling the effects of it. It's time for me to go before I get worse."

His eyes grew worried, even little creases grew upon his brow.

"What is the worst that could happen?" he asked.

I shrugged, not wanting to tell him about how I once read a journal entry about a Librarian who got stuck in another time and got so ill she wasn't able to travel back. When another Librarian came to find her, she was hospitalized for weeks and lost her ability to travel again. Her brain damage was so severe that life for her was altered permanently.

"I don't want to stick around and find out, Eoin. But, I am thankful to you. I am happy I met you. I feel —"

What did I feel? I thought for a moment, looking around at the beautiful hidden cave and the rushing blue water that cascaded down. "I feel grateful for you. For this opportunity. I'll never forget you."

His face smoothed out and he grasped my shoulders. "And I shall never forget you. Every time I see a thistle, I shall think of you and our travels. I don't want you to be ill. That's the last of my intentions, but I do wish to know you longer. Perhaps you can ride back to the castle with me. And we will have supper. Then you can go. Properly."

I thought on it for a moment and then nodded. I

didn't see the harm in having dinner and it would give me a chance to say goodbye to Iona.

"Okay. But right after supper."

Sixteen

The smell of smoke hit us about a mile away from the castle. Eoin kicked his monstrous horse and we rode as fast as the horses would go toward it. The whole time Eoin kept saying, *chan eil,* over and over. It meant *no* in Gaelic. I said nothing, even as the dizziness came back and hit me about three minutes out. I just shoved berries into my stomach, hoping that would keep the time sickness at bay. It did for a short time. When we reached the archway of vines, I knew something was horribly wrong. The thorns that had once been there had pieces of flesh embedded in them and they were lowered significantly. No longer did they cover our heads.

"These were up higher," I whispered.

"Aye, they were a warning. When an outsider comes into camp, they are lowered at the gate. It seems whoever entered got themselves a nasty scratch or two." he said, pointing to the sight of blood on the ground. My stomach turned. I didn't care for blood, I never have. I wasn't cut out for pools of blood on the grass or anything that involved torn flesh.

"Stay behind me, Savannah. Whoever it is, still may be here."

He pulled his bow and nocked an arrow, keeping it up and pointed ahead of him as his head was on a swivel. Only his legs clung to his massive horse, showing me the strength he must have had in them. Eoin was strong and I didn't doubt his advantage in a fight; I just didn't want to see it.

We reached the end of the archway and saw the destruction within. The smoke we saw came from the castle itself. All that was left was cinders and a smoldering smoke that grew up into the heavens. The once beautiful castle was now nothing. My mouth was open in shock and I couldn't close it. People lay around us, dead. Burnt or murdered by someone horrible.

"Iona?" I cried out.

"No, lass. Be quiet," Eoin yelled, but it was too late. I ran around the smoldering castle toward what would be the kitchens, searching for my friend. I found her crumpled up in a ball near the bath house. She was gone. Burns covered most of her body. I lay next to her on the ground and pulled her hair free from her face. She looked peaceful, not scared. Hopefully in death she was as free as she looked now. I swallowed the hard lump that formed in my throat. My poor friend had been brutally killed and I wasn't here to help her.

The anger of what happened here hit me tenfold. I stood up and faced Eoin, who was still watching the trees that surrounded us.

"Who would do this?"

He looked at me. "We've many enemies. But there is only one that would burn and murder my people like this. The English."

Bastards!

"Where is Ainsley?" I asked, searching for her in the wreckage. Stopping, I thought back to my research and she did live longer than Sir Malcolm, but then again, the text about him was wrong. They said Sir Malcolm would die by the hands of the English in 1304, and that didn't turn out to be true, did it? What historians wrote as fact wasn't always true, which was why we Librarians exist.

"She must be here somewhere," I told Eoin. "She won't die here."

We began to search the grounds for her, or any survivors, but we found nothing. It was possible that her body was inside the fire pit that was once a castle.

Eoin's head snapped up out of nowhere, and he pulled me behind him.

"What?" I asked, looking around.

"Shh, say nothing."

I didn't see or hear anything. It was just Eoin being panicky. But wait, what was that? I pulled my glasses free from my bag and I saw them. Ten soldiers riding toward us the same way we came in. Their leader looking entirely too happy as he surveyed the damage that lay at our feet.

"Good day, man. Nice day for a fire, isn't it?" he asked, riding in a large circle. Eoin's bow was up and trained on him. "Now, what is a strapping man like you and a pretty thing like that, doing here? Shouldn't you two be off frolicking in the heather somewhere? Making babies in the sunshine?"

I wanted to throw a rock at his face, but I stayed where I was. Eoin would get us out of this situation, I didn't doubt it.

"What's your name, young man?" the English soldier asked.

"*Chan innis mi dad dhut,*" Eoin replied.

"Well if you're not going to tell me anything, then I'll have to string your lassie up, like I did the other pretty redhead in this camp and do as I did to her. And let me tell you, lad, she didn't last long after we were all finished with her."

Eoin's arms began to shake, but not with fear, with adrenaline. This was a horrible situation to be in and I didn't see any good way out of it. My apprehension of seeing Eoin in a fight was coming to fruition before my very eyes. I suddenly felt the fear of losing him, like I lost Iona.

"You'll not be touching her," Eoin growled, his voice shaking, but strong. "I'll shoot you in the eye before you dismount yer horse. And then I'll shoot your friend to the right in his throat, and the next in the face. I've a good shot, and ten arrows. One for each of ye."

I was shocked when they all began laughing. I didn't think Eoin was joking. His family, or what was left of them, were all dead around his feet, and he was ready to kill someone. They had brutally murdered them all, of that there was no doubt. And Eoin wanted to make them pay. He was now all alone in this world.

"I believe you, man. I can see that you have a good hold on that bow, and a fine arrow you have there. But let me tell you what I think," he said, still on his mount. "I think you came back from a small trip, to find your whole camp massacred, by me and some one hundred men, and you're angry. I understand, good sir. But we came here to find someone, and we didn't find him. But we *did* find his bride, Lady Ainsley. You'll be happy to learn that she is well kept in a nice English camp just south of here. She's locked up nicely and that's where she will remain."

He kept circling us and all the while Eoin kept his aim,

and I stood behind him, helpless. I wished I had something more than the rocks at my feet. What good would that do me? You don't bring a rock to a sword fight.

"She was very open with us, indeed. She told us all about how Malcolm had died at his hideout, a place we never thought to look. But then she freely told us about his bastard son. And you know what, lad?"

Eoin said nothing, nor did he take his eye off his target. But I practically frothed with anger.

"I think that son is you! And you do know that I mustn't return to my king without Malcolm Walsh's head on a pike. His very last words to me were, 'Vargis, you get that son-of-a-bitch back to me so I may hang him in front of his very people for his crimes. Or you cut his head from his body! But either way, you bring him back.' Now I cannot go back without your father's head. So, I went to his lover's cottage, and do you know what I found?"

"What?" Eoin asked, rigidly.

"His burnt remains, but no head. What am I to do, bastard son? I cannot take ashes to my king."

Suddenly, it all came rushing back to me from all that I studied before this trip. Vargis was the man who captured Sir Malcolm and delivered him, alive, to the King of England. He was also the one who became a decorated hero because of it. And now, all this questioning, I realized something I hadn't before; the historians never got it wrong. They did hang Sir Malcolm Walsh for his crimes against England, except that it wasn't Sir Malcolm Walsh, it was Eoin. And with him slightly resembling his father, I could see how the English didn't suspect a thing. How could they know what Walsh really looked like?

Everything suddenly went into slow motion. The English soldier slowly began dismounting his horse at the same time as the other nine soldiers. Eoin did in fact loose his arrow, but as it flew through the air, I knew I had a choice to make. I could either stand here and watch as Eoin's arrow missed his target, and he is grabbed and taken away from me to pay for the crimes of his father, or I could save his life, and change everything, including the past; something I firmly believed was wrong. Changing history was not what we Librarians did. We observed, we did not intrude or for God sakes, alter.

"Screw it," I said, as I put the bracelet on my wrist and grabbed onto Eoin's arm, tightly. I felt the whooshing sensation, the power of the bracelet and the time-traveling formula it held, and heard the music in my ears, as we were pulled back in time, from this era to 2018.

****

At first, I lay there breathlessly. I felt the warm sensation of fur beneath me, and then I smelled the scent of warm cookies nearby. Not wanting to wake or open my eyes, rather, I stayed this way, just breathing. What I had been through, where I had just been, had defied all logic and explanation, and my body was paying the price. It was exhausted.

I could hear gasping next to me and I tried to ignore it and just rest, but the sound went on. I lifted my head and saw that the room would not stop spinning no matter how hard I tried.

"Ugh," I moaned.

"Savannah, stay very still. I have help coming. Just don't move." It was Jessa and I felt her nervous tension floating in the air, but I couldn't help ease it. I was too tired. "We will get you both some help. Just hold on." Her hand reached mine and she squeezed, tightly.

"Where am I? What on earth is this place? Savannah, what have ya done to me, lass?"

I knew the voice and I knew his questions needed answers, but I was too busy blacking out to answer them.

Seventeen

"**What you've experienced was a** total body shut down," the woman told me. She was dressed smartly, holding a worn book tightly in her arms. Her curly hair was pulled tightly into a nice low ponytail that showed off her kind face. "I myself have felt a sickness like this. But your illness is much worse than mine ever was. You'll need rest, which may be hard for you to hear because of your new visitor, and his questions."

She looked over at Eoin as he sat in my overstuffed chair. He was still dressed in his kilt and heavy quilted clothing, despite the warm room we were in. He looked terrified and I wasn't sure if it was shock of where we were or for me.

I was in my bed, at home, with Freddy wrapped practically around my face. I pushed her off, but she just went right back. Stubborn cat loved me too much.

"You do know you've broken our most sacred of laws, Savannah," she asked. "You are not to bring anyone from another time to ours. Think of the damage it could cause. The altered life that he will have."

"Yes, but you don't understand, they were going to hang him. If I left him there, he'd die for his father's crimes. He was innocent. I don't care what his—" I tried to go on but the damned cough I had now wracked through my body in spasms.

"Shh... try not to talk," she said. "I can't say that I didn't break a few rules myself as a Librarian. But this isn't your first go around. You rest, and we'll get him sorted out."

Turning to Eoin, she sat down on the edge of my bed. "You understand that you are a visitor in the 21st century? Your days are no longer and there are many things you will not understand. You're going to have tons of questions. Most of our world and our ways will come as a major shock to you, Eoin. I hope you're prepared for that."

Eoin nodded and looked at me with sadness in his eyes. "Will she be well soon?"

"She will. But she has to rest. Her body has traveled through time and stayed there too long. You'll do her good by not asking her all your questions. Anything you have to ask, you can ask me. My name is Emmeline, or Emme for short. Now, let's let her sleep and go into the next room to speak."

I looked at Eoin, and he at me. I didn't want him to leave, but I knew he had so many questions he was dying to ask them. Besides the concern that showed, he was comforting, and if he left, I would be lost again. If he was sent back, I'd go crazy.

"I just want to stay with her a moment," he told Emme. "And I'll meet you there, lass."

Emme smiled and got up. Jessa followed her out and closed the door behind her. Eoin looked around my room in wonder. He touched the stuffed bear on my bookshelf, and then ran his fingers across the books themselves. Picking up a few of my photos made him smile and shake his head. I could only imagine what was going through his mind as he looked at photos of me with Jessa.

"Everything is so full of color in your quarters. I cannot explain the feelings I'm having, just by standing here now. I feel... as if I do not fit here."

I laughed, and the damn cough came back. "Sorry, for laughing at you. You don't exactly fit in, Eoin. You come from another century. Your people are all gone. The days of Highlanders and clans are over, and the English did their damage, even after your war with them. But the fighting is all over."

His brows rose up as he asked, "The fighting is over? What do you mean, lass?"

"I mean that Scotland and England united, and there is peace. I promise you your country is no longer in turmoil." I sighed. "Eoin, do you understand why I pulled you back here?"

He nodded and sat down at the edge of my bed causing it to sink down a bit. I must have looked terrible. Freddy wouldn't stop climbing over my hair, and I felt like I'd hit a brick wall.

"I do, lass. I think that those men meant to hang me, and say I was Sir Malcolm. They wouldn't have stopped coming after me until they had me in their clutches. What you did was a great service. You saved me."

"But you don't belong here," I said, as I felt the tears well up in my eyes.

"No. I don't. There is something I must confess to you, Savannah." He bit his lower lip and fidgeted with his cloak. "Remember when you said that you don't feel as if you belong anywhere, like you're lost?"

I nodded. I remember that moment well. I recalled

how he told me that I was like the sun, and that there was a goodness in me that he felt he needed. The feeling we both desperately needed in our lives, we gave one another. And even in such a short time together, we had found an anchor in one another. He opened my eyes to a great many things and I could give him happiness, even for a brief moment. Maybe pulling him here was a blessing.

"Yes, how could I ever forget the talk on the mountain range?" I smiled.

He wiped the hair free from his eyes and took a deep breath. He was visibly worried about something. Then I began to panic slightly. Would Emme be taking Eoin back with her tonight? Is this the last moment I had with him?

"It's okay, Eoin," I said, as my voice shook. His hand gripped mine tightly. "You can tell me."

"I have never found a lass like you. I see much in you that reminds me of my ma, and I like that about you. But you're different than her in many ways, as well. You're much braver than she. She was afraid to fight for something she loved. And you, well, you look fear in the face and you laugh. You give me hope, something I never felt before. I need hope in my life, Savannah. And no matter where I am now, whatever the time, you're here. I cannot go back without you. *Mo cluaran*. I would be haunted with the memory of you in every step I walked."

This was nothing like what I thought he was going to say. Happy that he said this, I lifted my head, as high as I could, and grabbed his collar, pulling him down. It was now or never, but this kiss was going to happen.

His lips gently touched mine, and he pulled away for a moment, no doubt making sure I was all right.

"Nay lass." He pulled me from the bed and cradled me in his lap, instead of crushing me with his whole body.

I didn't fight it. As his lips met mine, this time in a more fervent kiss, it was as if the world around us went silent.

I wrapped my arms around his neck, and he held me tightly, running his fingers through my hair. He explored my mouth with his tongue, sending shockwaves through my body, awakening my senses. I felt things I had never felt before in this moment, and realized, Eoin was an amazing kisser. I also realized no one had ever kissed me like this before. His hands ventured, but never too far. His body shook with what I could only assume was passion, as I felt it too. If I wasn't exhausted, I would be doing more than kissing him.

When we finally came up for air, I realized that this could go no further than right here. I wanted nothing more than to fully explore Eoin in all ways possible, but we were not alone.

"I thought that kiss would never happen," I admitted, as my lips stung.

He chuckled. "I meant to kiss you many times, lass. But for fear of you slapping me, I stayed away, ever being the true polite Scot."

He laid me back onto the bed and covered me with the blanket. I felt empty and cold not being in his arms.

"I wish I could stay here with ya. But I think yer friends mean to have a serious talk with me," he said, with a jovial laugh. "I will return."

He left the room and I was alone with my thoughts. Many were of what had just occurred, but the others were of my future and if Eoin had room in it. Would he ever learn to accept this world that I lived in now? He was alone in Scotland before me. Ainsley was now gone and the camp was burnt to the ground. But if I learned anything in my reading, it was that Scottish men hold their pride and their honor above all else. As I closed my eyes to rest, I could only think of one possible solution for our situation and it wasn't what I wanted at all. But Eoin had to go home.

Eighteen

"**E**oin has to go back to Scotland," Jessa said, as she helped me dress. "It's been two days and he's completely lost, Savannah. He doesn't fit in here and I can't blame him. He wanders around the apartment like a lost puppy and Emme and I don't quite know what to do for him. We've filled him in on all things 21st century. Well, as much as we can. He's watched a lot of videos on YouTube about the fate of his people and Scottish history. He sure does love YouTube. I found him watching a kitten video over and over again, laughing like a buffoon. It was pretty cute."

I shook my head, and tried shoving her off, frustrated.

"I can dress myself, Jessa. I am feeling a lot better today. You don't need to be right here."

I was thankful for her help, but I was going stir crazy being cooped up in this apartment. Eoin and I had zero time together since our kiss and I wanted time alone with him. Jessa was helping me get ready, so we could go for a walk. Fresh air was good for me and it was what Emme said I needed. She had driven all the way down from Maine to help Jessa. It was smart of Jessa to find her when she knew I was lost. Instantly I felt bad for being fresh with her.

"You have no idea what it was like for me when I knew you were gone," she explained to me earlier in the day. "I was frantic. Sick. I looked to the guidebook and it hardly spoke about a traveler being lost and even less about what I should do to help. So I pulled out the index and Emmeline was the first number on there. Thank God she picked up the phone. The poor girl's planning a wedding and she stopped to help us. She's got a lot of knowledge, you know? She had her own experience being lost in time. But it was her choice to take off her tether."

"Sorry for snapping at you," I said to Jessa, shaking off the memory. "I know you went through hell to help me. I love you girl. I just... I don't want to lose him. I feel something with Eoin. Something I've never felt being around any other guy. He grounds me. I feel like I belong somewhere."

"Somewhere? What does that mean?"

I sighed. It was hard to explain this to someone who already found her place in this world. She belonged everywhere she planted her feet. Telling her the truth meant possibly hurting her feelings.

"It means that when I am with him, I feel like I belong with him. It doesn't matter where we are, we are whole when we are together."

She sat back against the wall, in shock. "You... you have feelings for him? You were gone for a little over two weeks, Savannah. How does one fall in love in that time frame?"

I guess the days blended together well enough that I didn't keep track of the time as well as I thought I did. But time meant nothing to me anymore.

"People fall in love at first sight, Jessa. It's actually possible to gain feelings in a two week time span. Besides you have no idea what we went through together on our journey to find this," I said as I held up my bracelet. "We learned a lot more about each other than I ever did about Trevor. He's a pure heart, Jessa. And I can't say that I don't feel a strong connection to him. I won't lie about that."

Her mouth closed and she grabbed me into a hug. "I'm so happy you're home. I was lost without you. I had to lie to everyone and say that you went on a trip to 'find yourself.' " I laughed, because that's exactly what I did.

"I missed you, too. I am glad you had Emme to keep you sane."

Speaking of Emme, I needed to hurry up and finish up here. She was leaving today and wanted to talk to me first. I brushed my hair, ran some product in it, and put on my glasses.

"I have a class," Jessa announced, as she looked at her watch. "I gotta run. See you guys later?"

I heard the tone in her voice, the one that said '*You're not going to run off to Scotland again are you?*'

"I have to stop off at the library to try to get my job back, and then we will be right here when you get home from class."

We said our goodbyes and I found Emme sitting in the kitchenette drinking freshly brewed coffee. I poured myself a glass, not realizing until then that I missed it beyond belief. She smiled up at me and I sat down across from her. She was a young Librarian, like me, who had loved someone from the past before. She told me her story last night. He was from England and she fell for him instantly. But she knew he was better off living his history, and not being with her. She had a duty to uphold, so she gave up their romance to save him and her library.

She was now engaged, and happy in her life. Her life as a Librarian came first, and she stayed true to her gift. I, on the other hand had started out the complete opposite. The gift was all I thought about. It was mine and no one else's. But like she said, I broke a cardinal rule. You never interfere. I had done so much damage.

"So how bad is it?" I asked her. She knew the meaning. I didn't have to explain to her.

"Sir Malcolm Walsh was never hanged for his crimes against the crown. They instead brought his ashes from his mistress's home and put them on display in the courtyard for all to see. They claimed that it was English soldiers who burnt him, and in the end that is what caused his death. They tied that in nicely with the fire at his former encampment. The original story was that they burnt down the castle, with him in it, but historians later proved that he was killed elsewhere. And that the English lied, about yet another thing. So, it's not bad, not at all."

I sighed as relief washed over me. "No, not bad."

"But you did break a rule. And he doesn't fit in here. You have a big decision to make, Savannah."

"Yeah, take him back and the English never stop hunting him until they get his head on a pike. The whole story about Sir Malcolm will change. And you know it. They'll kill Eoin instead."

She nodded and took a drink from her coffee. "Or you keep him here, and he is eternally lost in time, like you were. It's a conundrum."

"Sure is."

I saw her off to her car shortly after that and waved her goodbye then went into the apartment to get ready for my walk with Eoin who was waiting for me on the couch.

The girls had found a nice outfit for him to wear. Jessa did what she did best, found clothes to dress someone up in. I swear she should follow her passions.

"You look nice," I said to him. He stood up and turned toward me. His hair was brushed out and lay gently in waves across his back. I never realized how long it was.

"You as well," he said. "I hate these clothes. They itch. I miss my kilt. It's much freer and open. In this," he said, referring to his jeans. "They make me feel, well, confined. It's likely I'll die of strangulation if I stay in these."

"Strangulation of what exactly?" I asked with a giggle. His cheeks reddened and he laughed boisterously.

"Aye, I think you get my meaning and I don't have to explain it to ya. All the same, I miss my clothes, but I don't miss certain other things. Like being chased by the English soldiers. It feels like I can breathe for the first time in years. I don't have to be looking behind me as much. Waiting an ambush or an attack. Ye get my meaning?"

I did get it. That month away, I felt the same. The fear of being hurt or worse by the English weighed heavy on my mind.

"I heard your talk with Emmeline," he confessed as he approached me now. "I don't need ya to discuss what I plan on doing with her, lass. And ye don't have to worry about me neither. That's my decision, ye know."

I nodded. "I am sorry for talking about you when you weren't there to defend yourself. But she's right about some things, Eoin. If you go back the English soldiers will not stop hunting you until they have what they want. And if you stay, I'm afraid you'll never be happy here. Our world is much harsher than yours was. But not in the same ways. It's socially harsh. People are rude and can be mean at times. The ways of your people are lost, especially in America. We are selfish people and a lot of us only think of ourselves. Don't get me wrong, there are good people still to be found. But the unity of your people isn't the same as my people."

He stopped in front of me and took my hands in his and looked them over. Our hands fit well together, I noticed. Even though his were much larger and rougher than mine, they felt right. It hadn't been a long time that I'd known him, and there was so much more I needed to learn about him, but so far, I liked what I knew.

"I'll stop ye right there," he said, looking me in the eyes. "I make my own ways in this world, your time or mine, lass. And I've seen harsh things in your world, I seen a lot of your worlds moving pictures. It is scary here, that I will admit, but then there is beauty that I've never seen before. I miss Scotland so much I feel as if my heart will wither up without the smell of heather and the way the sun hits the grass in the mornin'. But seeing your face right now, it makes me happy. Happier than I ever was before. I make the choices for where I want to be. And I want to be with you. No matter where that is. I am not leaving here. You can try to take me back, but I won't go."

My breathing stopped as well as my heart. He was faithful to me? But why? Just like Jessa had pointed out, we barely knew one another. Yet, he was so willing to be here, in my time, to give up his world for me.

"You've only known me a short while Eoin. How can you say that?"

He kissed me in answer and held his arms around my body so gently, as if not to break me. When he pulled away, he said, "Did you feel that?"

I did feel it. The electricity of our connection, the passion, and the way I longed for more when he was finished.

"I did. What is it?"

He laughed and shook his head. "The people of my clan call it *anam-charaid*, or soul friend. It means that your soul has met its match. I believe that my soul has met its match in you, Savannah. From the moment my eyes fell upon you, I knew. I fought it but it's not worth the fight any longer."

There was once a time when I would have laughed at such a notion, but not anymore. I knew what he meant, because I felt it too. Although we were far from being in love or saying such deep words to one another, I did feel like my soul was meant to be with him. Our souls were matched and that's why I couldn't let him die in that field. It was also why I knew what we had to do.

"We have to go back to Scotland, Eoin," I voiced. "We have to try to save Ainsley and the others. It's crazy and it may not work, but I think we can go back and try to prevent the castle from being burned down. Maybe then I can feel like I accomplished some sort of goal as a Librarian. I was given this gift to observe history, and I broke a sacred vow by bringing you back. But nothing says that I can't save the lives of hundreds of people who are about to die needlessly. I want to go back and warn them at least."

"Aye, a fighting chance. And then what of us?" His eyes searched mine.

"I'm not sure where we will end up, Eoin. But I do know that I won't leave without you. This time I'm going to play it smart and safe."

He only nodded and took my hand in his. "I'll follow you then."

Nineteen

We took a walk around my neighborhood, allowing Eoin and I some much needed fresh air. Planning our trip back in time during our walk helped us visualize what we had to do. Eoin walked next to me, his hand in mine, as we spoke. Things with him were easy, and I felt comfortable, but I couldn't let my feelings cloud the duty and responsibility I had to face.

I had to do things right this time. I couldn't go into the book like I did last time; unprepared. This time I would be ready to face whatever the English soldiers had in store for us.

"Is there anything you haven't done that you want to do here? Before we head back," I asked as we reached the steps of my apartment.

"Hmm... I have taken a bath. But I don't understand the standing bath."

I looked at him sideways. "The shower?"

"Yes. I'd like to try a shower."

Showing him how to control the showerhead and the water, was the easy part. Hardest for me was resisting the urge to jump in the shower with him. I was never comfortable naked, but something about Eoin made me not even bat a lash at the thought. I wasn't an experienced girlfriend in the least, but there was an urge to be with Eoin in the purest of ways, that I'd never felt before. Sex was meant to be beautiful, and I couldn't help but think that Eoin would make it beautiful for me. He'd made me feel beautiful just being near him.

"Would you like to stay with me?" he asked, watching me, watch him. He took off his shirt, revealing a set of abs that practically made me squeal.

"Nope. No. I have things to do." He laughed as I closed the door, but before I did I caught a glimpse of him fully undressed. Thank God for the Scottish, because they made one perfect man.

After Eoin took his hot shower, which he said was amazing and wonderful, we headed to the library. I had to get my job back. Being gone so long had solidified that my future here was indeed bleak. Without a library to practice my craft, I was screwed. I needed the power of the library, and the books needed a safe place to be stored. Keeping them at home would never do. I made a vow to my grandmother that they would stay safe in the library's basement, and out of sight of prying eyes.

Eoin and I hopped in my car and after explaining to him why I drove instead of walked, and how the engine of a car worked, we drove down to the library. It wasn't far from our housing section of the college. We could have walked, but I was honestly afraid of how Eoin would feel about the people who milled around. To avoid any confrontation or weirdness, I figured driving was my best bet. I parked up front and Eoin followed my every move. He watched how I opened the car door, and how I closed it. It became a tad bit annoying after he even began walking like me.

"Eoin," I said, facing him. "You don't need to do everything I do. Just act natural."

He sighed, "Don't ye forget I don't know how to act natural in this world, Savannah."

Of course, he was right. I was just nervous and on edge.

"Sorry," I said. We walked in to the library and the brightness of it hit Eoin's face. His face was full of wonder and longing to learn more about this fascinating place. It was like showing a child some new toy. Explaining the library's history and inner workings, Eoin all but drooled over the interior and the beauty of it all.

We walked into the entryway and ran smack dab into Trevor.

"Oh," he said, holding me up as I stumbled into him. "You're back! Jessa told me you went on a trip. I see you are... looking well." His eyes scanned over my outfit and then back up to my face.

"I'm feeling amazing, actually." It wasn't a lie. The best part was I didn't feel those butterflies in my stomach upon seeing his face. I was over Trevor Arnold, one-hundred percent.

"Pleased to meet you good man," Eoin said, to Trevor. Instead of letting Eoin stumble into a harsh introduction of Middle Age proportions, I intervened.

"Yes, this is my friend, Eoin. He's from Scotland," I said to Trevor. "This is Trevor Arnold. The star football player here at our school."

Trevor nodded to Eoin, his jealousy apparent, and of which I wasn't sure why. Maybe good old Trevor saw something in me after all? Of that I wasn't sure nor did I care either way.

"Well, we must be going. See you around."

I grabbed Eoin's hand and pulled him hastily away. We found a suitable spot for Eoin to sit and read a book on Medieval History, so I could have adequate time to talk to the director.

"I'll be right back," I told him. He assured me he wouldn't talk to anyone or get too lost, and I made my way to her office. After a quick thirty minute talk about why I would never be working for this library again, or getting a good reference, I made my way downstairs to collect my things. I found my books in the hidden room, where I knew that Jessa had kept them safe. I picked them up and tucked them in a nearby satchel that my grandmother had given me. Standing in this room for the last time was surreal. I had screwed up not only my future, but Eoin's as well. Going back to Scotland was not a hard choice now. Nothing else was keeping me here besides Jessa. I couldn't leave until I spoke to her. And I did promise to be there when she got home from class.

I found Eoin in the same spot, but this time, surrounded by giggling, hair-tossing girls. He was talking animatedly of Scotland and the perils of living in the dreaded age of the English rule. I sighed, wondering how he got himself into such a fine mess, and pushed my way through the group of women.

"Eoin," I said, breaking free of two blondes who rudely tried to hold me back.

"Oh, my fair lady has arrived," he said, pointing to me. Literally all their heads swiveled toward me and their eyes filled with such hatred. So this was how they wanted it was it? Fine. Two could play this game.

"Eoin, darling, it's time to leave," I swooned. His smile grew wider, and he stood up, pushing away the gaggle of hags nearest him. "Sorry lassics, but myself and Savannah are off it seems. Good fortune to you all."

"Come on you big sap," I choked out, pulling him free. As we broke free of the library doors, I turned to him, to see if he was looking back at his fans who adoringly watched from the windows. I found his eyes secured on only me. "You made some friends I see."

"Friends? Och, no. They're just curious lasses, is all. I think they liked my hair. They touched it all too much. Does it still fit your liking? Do I?"

I leaned in, pulling him closer and kissed him, hard. As we pulled away he said, "Aye, I think that you do."

"I lost my job," I confessed as we made our way to the car. "I have no job, and no library to conduct my travels. Which sucks, royally, but it isn't the end of the world, I guess. But now I don't know how to support myself."

"Not sure what sucks means, lass, but it's unfortunate. Perhaps it wasn't meant to be. Another position will suit ye better, no doubt. You did a fine job in the kitchens." Always the positive one.

"Well, that's awfully nice of you, Eoin, but in this time you don't make a lot of money working in the food industry. And as a Librarian, archiving is my life. It's my future, too, so doing it for a job was helpful. It was a way to make money and do what I loved. Now, having a different job is going to throw a monkey wrench into the mix."

He only looked at me funny, but then nodded like he understood.

"Would you like to try something delicious?" I asked him.

"Does it entail you and me alone?" he said, pulling me

toward him by the waist. "I would find that very delicious."

I laughed, "I would too, trust me. But this is something you eat."

"Well, I would like to try that." I shook my head and broke free from his grasp, even though I didn't want to.

Ice cream was my go-to desert whenever I was having a bad day. Carmine's Bakery and Ice Cream Shop was my favorite place to go for treats. It was a bit of a drive, farther than I would normally have driven, but today, Carmine's was necessary. Eoin and I drove through the mountains of North Carolina, weaving in and out of the beautiful scenery around us.

I showed him where the mill was and how it was the top earning mill of our area. He had many questions about the mountains and their people and how the mill was run. I did my best to fill him in on that part of history, but his questions were unending. Eoin was much like a child in my time. He knew absolutely nothing about how the world worked and explaining it was a task. I realized I had only so much knowledge on the subject myself. I still had so much to learn if I was going to teach him anything before we went back.

Finally, we arrived at the little pink house that had been transformed into Carmine's. Upon walking in I could smell chocolate and sweet caramel in the air. Eoin's eyes went wide when the smell hit him.

"What is that?"

"I have one question, Eoin Walsh, do you trust me?"

He licked his lips and nodded his head. "With my heart, lass."

"Good. Now go sit down and I'll bring you heaven."

I ordered the biggest most exquisite brownie sundae

that Carmine's sold. When the waitress brought it to our table, Eoin's eyes bugged out of his head. His mind must have been going crazy trying to figure out what on earth it was. I grabbed a spoon and tapped his. "Pick that up and dig in."

He watched me and then he did the same. When the ice cream hit his mouth, he squealed, and then moaned with delight. Who knew eating ice cream could be so sexy? I just laughed as each bite he took gave him a different facial expression.

"It's so cold, but so sweet. How do they keep it cold?" he asked with a full mouth.

"Freezers," I said, launching into a lesson on refrigeration. He nodded, fully intrigued and kept eating until he couldn't eat any longer. He tossed the spoon on the table and sat back rubbing his belly.

"Full?"

"Oh, ye've no idea how full my belly feels right now. I loved every bite."

I had succeeded in at least treating him to something wonderful before we left. I wasn't sure what would happen when we went back to Scotland, but at least Eoin and I had a good time together. As brief as it was.

****

"Why do you have to travel again?" Jessa asked for the third time. And for the third time, I explained how going back to warn them was the best solution for everyone. A history where Iona and all of those lovely people were dead wasn't one I wanted to keep written in the books. I pulled the book free of the satchel. The blue of the cover shone bright in the candle lit room we sat in.

"I've never attempted to pick a certain spot and travel back to it, but Emme did. She told me how she went back to change how she met her subject once. She just went back to when they first met and started over. I can go back before the English arrive and warn them all. Eoin and I have it all planned out. We talked it over all afternoon, Jessa. And with you here, you can keep an eye out for me."

She bit her lip, as if thinking it over, and then nodded. "Okay, but will you come back?" She asked me but looked at Eoin. "Or will you stay?"

Eoin shook his head firmly, "I learned much from my readings this afternoon. The history of Scotland is brutal. And I'll not have Savannah going back to stay there. It's much too dangerous a place for her. I'll see to it that she is back here safely, Jessa."

As he said that, it solidified any doubt I had of Eoin coming back to my time. He planned on staying and making sure only I got out. Which meant he would hang for his father's crimes against the crown. Well, that may have been the fate he wanted, but I would make sure he was long gone before the English arrived. Maybe Eoin could escape with Lady Ainsley, and they could go into hiding somewhere the soldiers would never look.

But Eoin was going back. And I would come home a lost girl, once again.

Twenty

Not having the need to go to the village this time around gave Eoin and I time to head straight for the castle. We would arrive well before the English soldiers would, making sure they didn't hurt any of our friends or burn the castle down. Eoin had changed back into his kilt before we left, which brought a huge smile to my face, and I back into the dress I had once worn.

The trip through the book was simple for me, but not for Eoin. He had a hard time with the shift of time and threw up once we landed firmly on Scottish soil. I helped him ease into the transition with breathing techniques that assisted me the first few times I traveled.

"I remember the feeling you're having," I told him, thinking back on my first time I traveled. "You feel a little off, but you'll come around."

"Thanks, lass. I think I'll be fine," he said, taking his hand and putting it firmly on mine. "We have work to do you and I."

That we did. Without horses, we walked the rest of the way from where we landed, which was about a mile in a heavily wooded area.

The castle came into sight finally and upon seeing it standing and not burning I felt hopeful. This was all going to work out. The only hard part was going to be leaving Eoin behind. But I forced that down, deep down, and kept walking.

We reached the archway, which was still intact, and unharmed. Once out of it we saw children playing, and men working. Women in the field and Iona picking herbs. I ran to her, breaking free of Eoin's sight for just a moment.

"Iona!" I called to her. She looked up at me and smiled.

"Ah, lass. Ye've come back. Did ye find what ye were looking for then?" Did I ever. I showed her my bracelet and she touched it gently admiring its beauty and originality.

"Oh Iona, I did. I found that and more. I think I found myself on that journey." It was the first time I had admitted out loud how much that trip with Eoin had taught me. I had found my bracelet, a match for my soul, and who I was as a person. Most people are never that lucky, and it wasn't lost on me.

I wasn't going to fight with my mother any longer. When I got back home I intended to mend our broken relationship any way I could. No more holding back and holding onto old history. She was my mother, and I would forgive her. Even if that meant nothing to her, I needed to at least say it to her.

I discovered that I was more than a Librarian. I was Savannah Preston, student, researcher, and history enthusiast. I would not only preserve books, but I would preserve friendships, relationships, and the love of life itself. The Librarian sect wasn't my only destiny. I was young, yes, but old enough to learn that life didn't revolve on one future. It was made up of a million possible options and a lifetime of discovery.

"I'm pleased for you dearie. Did you come back to work for us then?" A hopeful glee filled her face.

"I'm afraid not, Iona. But I promise to see you before I leave. First, Eoin and I must talk to Lady Ainsley. Do you know where she is?"

Iona told me that Ainsley could be found in the castle easily enough. Today was mending day and as Iona assured me, Ainsley would be involved in the tradition with her clan. Eoin and I found her just where Iona said she'd be, and we watched as she and the group of ladies mended shirts and dyed fabric for new ones to be made.

"Ah, if it isn't my weary travelers. How did the trip south go? I suppose ye didn't run into any trouble." She put her hands into a bucket of dye and pulled out a garment that was stained a beautiful blue along with her hands.

"Mistress, may we speak, alone?" Eoin asked, bowing to one knee.

Ainsley's happy face faded. "Eoin surely you can speak freely in front of friends, no? Ye see I'm busy lad. What is it?"

He looked to me and then back to her, worrying his lower lip. "We come with warning, Savannah, er, Mollie and I. We know a great danger that is to befall the castle. You must escape as soon as you can milady. The English are on their way here. They mean to burn down the castle and kill us all. They know my father's dead, milady. Please, I urge ye all to flee."

Ainsley's concerned face quickly turned to fright as she threw the garment down and stood fast. Her eyes held contempt and anger. I had never seen this before from her. Seeing the side of her that showed her abilities was completely different from what I saw now.

"How dare you come in here and whisper such lies, Eoin. What proof do ye have of such news?"

I was confused. How could she not take heed our warning? What on earth would make her think Eoin would lie about such a thing? Perhaps it was because he mentioned Sir Malcolm's death.

"He's telling the truth Mistress Ainsley. I've seen it with my own eyes. They are not far away. You have time though. Time to get everyone out, safely."

"Oh do I?"

I nodded, and then realized, she was mocking me.

"We are telling the truth."

"Ye've seen it? Seen what?" She eyeballed me and I realized my mistake. Telling her I had seen what was going to happen was making things worse now. The Scottish held true to their fairy lore and they were a highly suspicious people. Even though she claimed to be some sort of psychic, she didn't like the fact that Eoin and I knew something she didn't.

"I mean, we saw the English," I lied. "They make their way here, now."

"Eoin," she said, facing him. "How do you know they saw your father? Eh? Did they tell you that? Are you in league with them now? So set on destroying not only my marriage to the only man I'll ever love that now you tell the bloody English bastards where we are. Do ye hate me that much?" She spat on the ground near his feet. He backed up a step, shaking his head.

"No, lady. Hate ye I do not. I only wish to find a place in this world. I never intended to harm your marriage. I didn't ask to be born. He didn't even love me, ye know?"

She laughed wickedly and shook her head. What happened to the lovely lady I had spoken with just a few nights back? This was not the outcome I had hoped for. In fact, it was going much worse.

"Are you in league with the fairies then? Is that it? Or are ye a witch? I did find it odd how you just arrived in our castle, clear out of the blue sky. Like you dropped here. Did you come to bring the cursed English our way, then?" she asked, looking at me.

"Oh, absolutely not. I'm not a witch. I'm a friend," I urged. But before I could plead my case, I was grabbed up by two of Sir Malcolm's finest fighters. Ainsley ordered them to take me to the keep, which was where they held the prisoners. I had arrived here a friend and was now being thrown in a cell as foe.

As they pulled me away I could hear Eoin beg Ainsley for mercy, pleading with her for my very life. She wouldn't have it. And once I reached the corner, I heard her order him locked up in the tower. We were to be kept separate and there was no way I could help him.

Once the men threw me in the cell, I realized I wasn't totally out of luck. I had my bracelet still, and with any hope, the book would pull me back. I'd have accomplished nothing though. My trip would have caused nothing more than havoc. Eoin was locked up and the English soldiers were on their way. The fire would engulf this whole structure and this time, it would cause death to someone else I held dear.

The door slammed behind me and I didn't fight back or bang on it. There wasn't anything I could say that would change their minds. I had to figure out what to do.

I sat down on the floor, noticing that the keep wasn't as awful as I thought. My perception of a cell was dark and dank, but this was just a room, with a heavily bolted door. There were windows with bars, and that was awful, but they let in plenty of light. Knowing what I had to do to get out of this sticky situation seemed to calm my frayed nerves. The fact that Ainsley was so stubborn, angered me beyond belief. At least she knew they were coming, even if she did think we played a part in it.

"Jessa," I called out, hoping beyond hope that somehow through our bond, she could hear me. "I need to be pulled back. I'm in trouble."

Waiting and being patient was something I found hard to do. I was stubborn, and I wanted out of this predicament.

"Please, Jessa! Hear me. Hear me." I waited, and still nothing. Sitting back against the wall, I decided to wait. Eventually the book would pull me back, right?

It had to. A Librarian is guaranteed almost certain safety when danger arrived upon their missions as long as they had their tether. That's why we were given protectors who watched over us as we traveled. As I recorded the history, it was being rewritten word for word onto the blank pages of the book. When we get a mission, our book is blank, it's our journey and experiences that fill up those pages. But, since that part had already been rewritten when Eoin and I were here the first time, I wasn't sure if my coming back and trying again would alter it somehow. Would it all be word for word on the pages for Jessa to read? Or would it not show up, since I was breaking the rules? All I could hope was that Jessa was seeing it in real time, keeping me safe.

"Mollie." A whisper came suddenly from the door. "Are ya faring well in there?"

It was Iona. Of course she'd come to see if I was okay.

I leaned on the door, placing my hand atop it. "I'm all right. How's Eoin?"

"Fine, fine. I believe ye, dear. I don't believe you bring

us ill will. Mistress Ainsley isn't well. She's not been sleeping and I fear that the death of Sir Malcolm has disturbed her mind. It's placed an evil rot into it."

"How do you know he's dead?" I asked. I thought it was a secret that Ainsley held dear to her, never letting it slip.

She scoffed. "Most of us servants can hear many things in this castle, dear. I've known ever since Eoin arrived. He's the look of his father, he does. We've got to get you free of this room. I've brought help. But you need to be quick on yer feet. Can you do that?"

I nodded, lamely, and then said, "Yes."

The door burst open revealing Graham, the horsemaster, and a worried looking Iona. She pulled me into a quick hug, even though I'd only been locked up for a mere half an hour.

"What's the plan now?" Graham asked, trusting me.

"You need to warn as many as will listen that the English are on their way. They will kill us all. Be ready to fight and help those that can't to escape."

Iona thought a moment and then said, "I know just the place for them to escape to. There is a cave hidden beneath the falls of Fare Glen. It can hold all the women and children. I shall get them ready." If she was talking about the falls Eoin and I went to, then she was right. The women and children could fit in their safely until we got the English away. I silently prayed that it would work.

"And I'll get the men on the right side of the battle," Malcolm said, sternly. "We're not going down without a proper fight."

Twenty-One

Iona helped lead me through the castle as quietly as possible. Before rounding corners, we listened for any sounds of threat against our plans. We could hear absolutely nothing this deep in the castles interior. She was leading me through a part of the castle that only servants had entry to. It was how they stayed behind the scenes, doing all the chores necessary to keep the castle running. In history texts they don't talk nearly enough about the importance of servants. They really were the hidden figures of history. Without them the castle would be in disarray. The rich spoiled women like Ainsley would be lost without someone to heat water for her daily baths. I silently laughed at the visual of Ainsley heating her own water. What a thought. She'd probably have a heart attack if she had to cook her own food. I wondered how Ainsley went so wrong in life. Was it the death of Sir Malcolm that disturbed her mind, or was she like that all the time? Perhaps that's why Malcolm fell in love with Eoin's mom. His wife was mad and he fell for the beautiful lass on the edge of the wood. I didn't blame him in that case. It wasn't like divorce was legal. What did a man or woman do when their spouse was batshit crazy?

"Iona," I said, as we snuck around another corner. "Has Lady Ainsley always been mad?"

Iona nodded her head and said, "Oh aye! She can hold it in for a bit, but then the devil rears his ugly head in her eyes. When that happens, she is locked up in chambers until he goes away. When Sir Malcolm was at the homestead with her, he was better equipped, you could say, to handle her ravings. But now we just do our best to lock the devil away at night."

Well that answered that question. Ainsley suffered from a mental condition that the people of this time just thought was the devil at play. It was rather sad. And to think that I thought she was nice. Boy was I wrong. It didn't take her long to turn on me.

"Come up this way," she urged as we climbed up a set of stairs. "Your man is up there."

She pointed up to a walkway that opened outside.

"You want *me* to go up *there*? Are there guards?"

She shook her head, assuring me it was free of men at the present moment. They were apparently all busy protecting the castle from the oncoming English horde making their way here.

"They locked him up and left. They're all with Graham now, talking things over no doubt. They did as mistress said, locking you two up, then battle plans were put into place. They won't listen to her. Don't fret. Go rescue him." I hugged Iona tightly, not sure what would be our fate after I got Eoin free. I didn't even know if I was going to stay or if the book would pull me back.

"Thank you, Iona. You've been wonderful. I'll never forget that you did this."

She patted me on the back and then said, "Bah, now go. No more nonsense. I must be getting the women and children away from this castle." As coy as she played, I did see tears in her eyes.

I broke free from Iona and made my way up the steps. How funny it was that it was me saving Eoin, instead of the other way around. I guess women can save their men, too.

I took step after step and each one I made I realized how much Eoin meant to me. He had opened my eyes to so much in this beautiful world. Eating meat again was all due to Eoin. Making me feel beautiful in my own skin, again, Eoin. Believing in myself more, Eoin. And wanting to patch things up with my mom, still Eoin. Losing him would mean losing a part of myself that I had gained in knowing him. The very thought of leaving him here in this country to die would in turn kill me. Before I knew it, I had reached the top of the castle where a tall tower stood. I pulled the wood block free and the door swung open. Eoin turned, his hands up blocking the light, but revealing a severely damaged face.

"Oh my goodness, Eoin, your face! What happened?" I rushed in to grab him and he held me in his strong arms.

"Worry not, Savannah. They gave me a good thrashing, but I'll manage. Did they hurt ye?"

"No, I'm fine. They didn't lay a hand on me," I assured him, even as he looked me over. I placed my hand on his face, and he gasped. His eyes were bruised beyond belief. He could barely see out of the right, but the left was completely swollen shut.

"Assholes!" I cursed.

"Aye, now, don't worry about it. We must get free

of here. They're planning on a fight and I'll not have you caught in it. Let's get you back to your time and have ye safe at home with Jessa and that crazy feline of yours."

I laughed, but tears were streaming down my face.

He took his thumbs and brushed them away gently.

"No, don't ye cry, lass. I'll not have you shed a tear for me. You can come back to visit anytime ye want, right?"

A lump was forming in my throat and it made it almost impossible to speak to him without outright bawling. I had to explain to him what would happen to his book once I got back home. I looked down at my bracelet like a ticking time bomb that was counting down the very minutes that I had left with him. Unclasping it and putting it inside the top of my corset for safekeeping was the best thing to keep me here for now.

Eoin's eyes went wide. "Savannah, you cannot stay here. You've said it yerself. There is no winning this war right now. Not for a while, yet. You told me it does not get better for a long time. You wouldn't want to stay here for that, Savannah. You go back home and be with your friend. Be with yer ma and make things right between ya. Don't ye stay here where only certain death is to follow your very step."

Finally finding my voice I said, "You're right. In this world there is certain death. There's certain danger. But there is also something I never found in my time, and that's you. I finally feel like I belong. I don't feel lost anymore. In my time I'm walking around in a world I don't belong in. With you, I feel at home. So that's why I leave it up to you to make a decision, for me, for us. Don't think with your head, think with your heart."

His eyes went wide and he held me tightly, almost like he didn't want to let me go.

"What would that be? Because if you are asking me to have ye stay, I'll send you home."

"Do you not want me with you? Why? Because it's dangerous?"

He shook his head and resting his forehead to mine. "Nay. I want you here. More than I've wanted anything near me. My whole life I have never wanted anything like I want you. But I won't let you be here to have your life snuffed out like a flame."

My tears were flowing now and I couldn't stop them. He was sending me back. It was for my safety, yes, but he was still sending me home.

"Eoin, if I go back, I cannot ever come visit you. I'm required to seal the book on Sir Malcolm and send it to the archives. I won't be permitted to visit you. It doesn't work like that."

His face was twisted and his hands trembled. He was understanding that if he said goodbye, it was goodbye forever. Now he saw why this was so hard for me.

"You mentioned a choice?"

I did. "It's risky. But if it works, we can be together."

At that moment, before I could get another word in to explain I heard the shouts below of the English soldiers as they formed a circle around the castle. There were hundreds of them and only a mere hundred Scots hurrying to prepare for a battle they couldn't win. The prideful Scots held pitchforks, and a few swords for weapons, but the English were better equipped. With their horses, and their shiny armor and sharp weaponry they would wipe these men out no problem. From our view up top we could see what the men at the ground could not; they were seriously outnumbered and outranked.

"Oh shite, they're here," Eoin said, holding me close.

"Go now! Get back to your time, Savannah."

"I can't. I took off my tether. Even if I put it on the book might not pull me back quick enough." Sure, I was being stubborn but that was a lesson I took from Eoin's handbook.

I didn't want to go yet. I wanted Eoin to make a choice first, but that would have to await the battle brewing below.

Then a thought hit me that hadn't before. What if a battle never had to happen here? What if the English got what they wanted, and they just left. They had to want something, right?

"Do you trust me?" I asked Eoin, who looked at me sideways.

"I do. As crazy as ye are. I trust ye."

Twenty-Two

We walked down the cobblestone steps of the outer part of the castle making our way to the ground. If my plans worked well enough, there wouldn't need to be any blood shed on this day. Eoin had to do as I said, and not a thing different. I found a horse in the stable, and Eoin helped me up on him. I had changed into one of Ainsley's nicest dresses and did my hair up in the fashionable English way. I had to look the part if I was going to play the part. Playing the part was what I was used to as a Librarian. Blending in to fit the time period and the people surrounding it.

"Ride him slow," Eoin urged. "He'll buck ye off if you go too fast."

I nodded, remembering this wild stallion from the day I had arrived. His nostrils flared as I took the reins.

"He and I have an understanding," I said to Eoin and the horse. "Eoin, I'll be right back."

"I hope so, lass. You getting hurt would kill me." I leaned down and Eoin pulled me toward him, kissing me soft and slow. After we broke apart, his kiss lingered on my lips.

I rode past the Scots as they stood awaiting the English to pass through their archway of thorns.

They didn't see the view Eoin and I had. They had no clue how many soldiers were waiting just outside the archway and that they held no chance to survive.

Eoin talked to the men, letting them know I had an idea. As mad as it was, it just might work. I was willing to do anything to save these people and Eoin. The stallion and I rode through the archway, he bristled as I led him through it gently.

"Easy boy. I won't hurt you as long as you don't go throwing me off." We finally broke free and I saw the English soldiers who held up their weapons as I approached. I held up my hands, innocently, looking as appalled as possible.

"I have no weapons. I only mean to talk," I said. "Who's in charge here? And how dare you raise arms against me!"

When Vargis came forward I silently said a thank you to God above and then straightened myself up. The goal was simple, play the part, but my darn hands wouldn't stop trembling.

"Ah, Vargis," I said, with my best English accent. "It's good to see you again, cousin. How's Leticia? Is she doing well, then? I heard tell that she gave birth to a healthy son."

Vargis' eyes widened in surprise. But I just kept talking to keep him focused on me.

"Do I know you milady?"

I acted baffled. "Do you not recognize me cousin? Has it really been that long since we've seen one another?"

I had done some research while I laid in that bed for two days. Research was, after all, what I did as an archivist. This research was on one Arthur Vargis and his entire family. I knew we would need to know the devil we were fighting. It turned out Arthur Vargis was a family man. His wife, Leticia, a Scottish woman, was the love of his life. And his cousin, a red haired English noblewoman by the name of Olivia Vargis was a woman of means who went around Scotland and England raising money for the war. She was a very influential woman, who with her family's money, helped pay for a lot of the war. She ended up marrying a prince somewhere in another country, but if my plan was to work, I had to play the part. I did notice that beyond the red hair Olivia Vargis and I looked much alike.

"Olivia?" Yep. Bless my red hair. "It's been so long since I've seen you. Not since we were children. You've changed. What on earth are you doing here in this filthy Scottish pigsty?"

Yep that hurt, but I pretended that it didn't.

"Dear me, yes, this place is a disgrace. But you do know cousin that I travel looking for sympathizers to our cause. And these people, as foul as they are, know who their one true king is. They mean no harm. If anything, they are perfect servants for me. Hosting me as they do. I'm treated like a princess here. I must say, I'm shocked to see the king's men suited up and ready to fight against people who matter not."

Vargis' eyes searched his men and then looked at the castle. Maybe what I was saying wasn't fooling him, because he sure looked pissed. Or skeptical. Either way he looked unsure.

"Would you like a warm hearty meal for your men here? I am sure the kitchen wench could throw together a nice meal for you. Is it lodging you're searching for?"

Vargis coughed and then sat up straighter on his horse. "Nay. We are here searching for a murderer. I heard that he was here. But if you're here, surely he wouldn't be."

He bit his lip. Yep, he was unsure.

"Pray tell, me in the presence of a murderer? Surely you know me well enough to know I do not keep such company!" I scoffed.

"Yes, cousin. I do know you like to keep only good company, even if they are dirty Scot's." He spat on the ground. "If there is no such man here, I will be on my way. But first, I will search the grounds. Surely they have no issue with that?"

I shook my head. Crap! Having them come inside the grounds wasn't what I planned. This wasn't supposed to play out this way. He was supposed to trust me and my word and be on his way.

"Oh cousin, you doubt me? What do you think I am? A liar? Do we not have trust and faith in one another?" I had to turn on the charm, and real quick. So I fluttered my lashes and fanned myself. I scanned the crowd of soldiers and smiled at them all, looking demure and as innocent as possible.

"Sir, perhaps Malcolm isn't here at all. What would such a monger be doing in the presence of such a fine lady as your cousin?" A soldier in high standing asked.

"Olivia, you're not being held against your will, are you?"

My mouth fell open. "Oh surely not. If so how would I ride out here on my own? And on such a fine stallion." At the same moment the horse neighed proudly. It couldn't have gone any more perfectly than that. I loved that horse in that very moment.

"This lady is not a liar. That I can see," said the soldier. He hopped down from his horse, came close to me and kissed my hand. Then one by one several men did the same. After a while I began to be annoyed, thinking about all the germs I was coming in contact with. But I didn't break my smile, keeping up the ruse was the best thing I could do.

"May I ask whom you're searching for?" I asked playing coy.

"The ruthless killer Malcolm Walsh!" Vargis said, as he too kissed my hand. "Have you heard any rumors?"

I nodded. This was my shining moment. "Oh yes! I have. What a horrible mongrel that man was! The day we heard of his death, the whole castle celebrated with a feast of boar! And what a delicious boar it was. What a shame you're searching for a dead man, cousin. Did you not know?"

I knew that Vargis didn't know this news yet. He had learned it previously because Ainsley had told him as he tortured her. But that would not be happening, even if she was crazy. I would be telling him about the death of Sir Malcolm. As for what they would bring back to the king for proof, well I had a plan for that as well.

"Dead! How?"

"A fever took him and his lover. Such a shame that you didn't know. I hope you find his body and are able to string it up to show the people of our country what happens to murderers." I shook my head and tried to look menacing.

"Who told you this?" Vargis asked, still doubt in his voice.

"A Scot that was passing through trying to sell trinkets to the servants. He said that he had found the remains of this Malcolm fellow and ransacked his home for treasure. He didn't tell me personally, but the servants talk you see."

"What was this vagrant's name?"

I acted like I had to think about it for a while. I tapped my chin and then said, "Finn was his name I think. As for his last name I cannot recall. The ladies in the kitchen do like to talk, and you know I listen." Olivia was known for her rumors and her mouth, which I had just played almost perfectly. Jessa would be so proud of me and my acting skills.

"Landry, mark that name down. We will search for this Finn and we won't stop until we find him. If he knows where Walsh's body is, we can drag it back to the king."

There wouldn't be anything for them to find, because at that same moment that I was talking to these English soldiers, Eoin was riding to his mother's home to move their ashes to a better resting place. He was removing anything that could be tied to Sir Malcolm, so that his father and mother wouldn't be bothered. No one would think anything of their empty home in the woods. As for Finn, well he shouldn't have stolen from me. If the soldiers found him, then perhaps he'd be questioned and get the punishment he deserved for stealing things that didn't belong to him.

I only had to hope that this didn't alter anything too much for Sir Malcolm's history.

With renewed purpose Vargis got back onto his stallion, bid me goodbye and took his soldiers far away from the castle. I had done it! There would be no blood spilled today and the castle would remain unharmed.

I took the stallion and rode him back into the archway and straight to the stables. Graham met me and quickly helped me down.

"Lass, you're being searched for by Mistress Ainsley. If she sees you she'll likely kill you."

I shrugged, for once not caring what Ainsley had in store for me.

"Well, let her try. I can't worry about that crazy hag right now. I just saved all your asses from total destruction." Feeling quite the badass at the moment, I didn't care about

Ainsley or her idle threats.

So when Ainsley came up behind me with her hands on her hips, I was ready for her.

Twenty-Three

She looked beyond angry that I was not locked up like she wanted me to be. But I stood firm. If she only knew what I had just done for her and her faithful servants and followers of Sir Malcolm. She was ungrateful, and a tad psycho. I didn't have time to stand here and argue with her, I promised Eoin I would meet him near the waterfall. Maybe at that point we could say our proper goodbyes and then... then I didn't know what would happen. Just thinking about it broke my heart. It almost felt like I would be burying my heart and leaving it here in Scotland.

Love was complicated for me. I didn't have much of a history to account for. But with Eoin, the possibility of loving him felt easy. As easy as breathing. Or as easy as reading a book. It was peaceful and I wanted it.

"How did you escape?" she snarled.

"Wow, you sure changed. You are not the same lady I met with in your room, Ainsley. You are losing your mind, do you realize that?" I began, standing tall. "You almost got all these people killed today because you are falling apart at the very seams. And I get it. You lost your husband and it wasn't easy. But these people, they need you. And they need to know Sir Malcolm is dead. You can have a life without him. Your future is good, if you allow yourself to let others in."

The slap that came after about knocked me off of my feet. I'd never been slapped before. Wow it hurt. I tried really hard to not show how badly it stung, but the tears of anger filled my eyes and I was sure my cheek was bright red. I was trying to talk to her seriously and it seemed she didn't like that.

"Okay, then. So you want to play that way do you?"

She held her head high, Ainsley was a proud woman and would not admit her faults.

"Ainsley, I am leaving now and no one here is going to stop me. You do realize that I saved their lives, right?"

"Who are you?" she snarled. "Ye aren't who ye claim to be, that's for certain."

I laughed. "No, I am not who I claimed to be. I'm much more important than that. And I thank you for your lovely hospitality, I think the locking me up part was a tad much, but it's time for me to be leaving. And you will not stop me."

She moved aside, as if scared of me. Perhaps she thought of me as a threat. Before I left the stables she asked, "Are ye a witch?"

Turning on my heel I said, "Who knows? But one thing is for sure, if you do not start protecting these people better, I will be back and so will the English. Don't be stupid, Ainsley."

And in a surprising turn of events she fell to her knees and wailed like a baby. I didn't stop to look back at her. My job here was done. My mission had altered, but I had done what I set out to do, and then some. I saved Sir

Malcolm's people. And I liked to think that he was smiling down on me, thankful for what I had done for them. As I left the castle and said my goodbyes to all the men who would mostly die in the upcoming battles that lie ahead, I felt a release of pressure. I had saved them that day at least.

The walk to the waterfall wasn't long and I had done it before with Eoin, so it wasn't hard to find. I didn't see Eoin, so I went into the cave where Iona and all the other women were with the children.

"It's safe," I told them all. Their eyes lit up. "You can all go home now. Be safe."

"Thank you, child," Iona told me. "Will I ever see you again?"

Sadness crept over me as I told her, "No." But I knew Iona would be all right. If anyone ran that castle it was she. She hugged me for the last time and wished me safe travels. As they all walked away, I watched them until the sun began to lower in the distance. Eoin should have been here by now, but he wasn't.

Thoughts of him getting caught flooded my brain and I couldn't help but think the absolute worst for him. Instead of waiting in the cold cave I wandered out and tried to find the best spot to be able to see him if he crested the hill. Finding the perfect rock high up allowed me the sight to see all over.

I sat down on it, my legs tired, and noticed that I had found the most beautiful patch of thistles. I had actually never seen them growing wild before, but as I sat down I saw they were spreading all over this hill. I plucked one and then another, until I had enough for a flower crown. Braiding them together helped ease my mind. When the crown was done, I sat it atop my head.

"That looks bonnie on you."

Gasping, I looked up and saw Eoin holding his own bouquet of flowers in his hands. They were thistles too.

"You're late," I teased.

"Ah, sorry lass, I know. 'Twas hard saying goodbye again to my parents. But on the walk to meet you I stumbled across a patch of these and I wanted to pick them for ye. But I see that you found your own."

His smile lit up his face but didn't disguise the red eyes he had from shedding tears. I patted the grass near me and he dropped down in a heap.

"You missed it," I told him. "I told Ainsley off."

He cocked his head.

"Uh, I mean to say we had words. She slapped me," I said, as I showed him my face. "It hurt."

"Aye, try being hit with a fist."

He held up his fist and then uncurled his fingers and ran that hand over my face.

It was now or never. The part I was dreading.

"Eoin, I don't want to leave. I..."

"Shh lass. I know. But what if you didn't have to leave. What if ye gave me a choice?"

"A choice? I don't understand."

He looked around at his beautiful country and then back at me and touched my face once again.

"If ye ask me if I want to wake up in this land every day of my life, I'll tell ye yes. But if you ask me if my heart will ache every day you are gone, I'll say yes again. Isn't there a way I can be with you? A way I can wake up next to you every day and see the land I love?"

I felt the same way about him, but I couldn't stay here. This land was beautiful but so full of tragedy. How many years would we have without death or pain? I couldn't leave behind my time. I had so many things I still needed to do back home. For instance, my best friend and the way I left things with my mother.

"I have broken pieces back home. But I'd have a broken heart if I left you." I put my head in my hands. I didn't know what to do. He pulled me off of my rock, and onto his lap, where I curled up like a child. Sadness did that to you. It made you act like a broken innocent kid. I didn't want to make decisions right now.

"Aye lass. I have broken pieces, too. Let's be broken together."

And before I knew it I understood what he meant. I raised my head and asked the question that had been on my mind for days, but I was just too scared to ask.

"Eoin, do you think that you could love me?"

This was the hardest question I had to ask anyone before. I was putting my heart out there; it was vulnerable.

He kissed me and took my face in his rough hands. He pulled me back onto the grass and he lay with me, holding me. Love. This was what it felt like. Two people intertwined together.

He lifted his head and said, "I'd go anywhere with you, lass. And as for yer question, I already do."

I sat up and looked out at the beautiful Scottish landscape that I was about to say goodbye to for now and then looked at Eoin.

Without any words, or any further questions I held out my hand to him. He took it and we stood up. I pulled out my bracelet and put it back on.

We were standing in my bedroom seconds later. Eoin had grass in his hair, and I held onto the flowers he gave me but my crown was gone. Oh well, perhaps a child would find it. At least a piece of me was still there.

I was scared to look at Eoin, for fear of him looking sad that he had left Scotland to come here with me. What would happen to us if he realized his mistake and wanted to go back home? Would I be able to live without him? Knowing what I knew now, in that moment, that I had fallen so hard for someone so fast, I couldn't be without him.

"Look at me, lass," he said. So I did. "I would follow you anywhere; I told you that. I made this choice."

"Eoin, I have an idea, but I need you to trust me. Do you?"

He pulled me into my arms, and kissed me, which I took meant yes. All of the times that I faked being happy in my life, this time was different. My happiness with him was genuine. Sure, our relationship was complicated and he had just given up his time for mine, but he would see Scotland again soon.

Twenty-Four

O ur flight was leaving at two o'clock and we were already packed and ready to go. Jessa was our cook for breakfast apparently, because she had a full meal laid out for us when we rolled out of bed. She was merrily humming as she placed bacon on the counter and filled our glasses with orange juice.

"Wow, Jessa, this is quite the spread," I remarked, as I sat down at the table.

She waved her hand dismissively. "It was nothing. I love to do it, you know that."

I nodded as I flung pancakes onto my plate and doused them in syrup. I would miss surprise breakfast from Jessa, it was the only thing she knew how to make. As for me, I couldn't make anything. I'd have to learn if I was going to feed Eoin.

He was still getting dressed so Jessa and I had a few minutes to ourselves.

"Jessa, I want you to know that you and I will always be friends, even now that Eoin and I are going to Scotland. I'll never have another friend like you. Ever."

She nodded and I saw her swallow. I knew that she was trying not to cry. It was the reason she cooked so much food, and why she sang all morning; diversion tactics.

Eoin and I had made the choice to move to Scotland so that he could be home, in a sense. Moving there was a no brainer for me. There was no place that made me feel more at home than Scotland and in Eoin's arms. Putting the both of them together made Savannah one happy girl.

"But I won't be your protector any longer," she said, sitting down with her smoothie, while shoving a piece of pancake in her mouth.

She was right. That was the only bad part of this move; losing her. We both knew that long distance friendships were hard. I'd need a new place to conduct my preserving and a new protector in order to travel. It was a thought that weighed heavily on me.

"I can do it," Eoin said, as he appeared in the kitchen fully dressed in his kilt. I sighed at the sight of him.

"You, protect her?" Jessa asked incredulously.

Eoin sat down, in the tiny seat next to me. He practically dwarfed anything he was near. Including our furniture.

"Why not? I will protect her with my body and my soul if I need to. Why can I not do so when she travels?"

"I don't see why he can't," I agreed, stuffing a piece of pancake in my mouth. "But Jessa will have to teach you, Eoin. Maybe we can Facetime and she can teach you then? She knows all the rules and is the only one I'd trust to be your tutor."

It seemed like a nice way to include Jessa, and Eoin did have a lot to learn.

"I am a good teacher," Jessa said.

"Aye, no doubt I'd be learnin' from the best. First

lesson, Facetime."

They both laughed.

I loved how my best friend and my boyfriend got along so well. And I can't believe I had a *boyfriend*. Using the word was foreign to me. But one night, when we were alone, I had asked him if that was what he was. He said, "I do not know the term. But if it means that I belong to you, then yes. I guess I am yer boyfriend."

They talked over breakfast as Jessa gave him his first rundown on all things protector. She excused herself from the table a few minutes later, and I began washing the dishes and putting the rest of the food into containers for Jessa to eat while we were gone. I realized that poor Jessa would be alone for a while. If anyone needed a roommate it was Jessa. She needed me as much as I her. I sat there with my hands in the water, watching the soap run over them, and the tears that fell from my eyes drop down into the soap. Ever since meeting Eoin, I was an emotional wreck. I cried all the time. Love does that I suppose. It sure brought out the side of me I tucked deep, deep down.

"What is it?" Eoin asked. I shook my head, not able to talk. "Ye don't want to leave? We don't have to. I can adjust here. I can live here with you. I can be happy in time."

I looked at him and had no doubt that he would do fine here. Eoin could blend in anywhere he went. He was already learning so fast in the past four weeks we had been back. He knew a lot about how the world worked, but heck, even I didn't know it all. There was so much that he didn't know, because I wasn't informed enough to teach him. Being in Scotland would allow him to feel comfortable enough to learn such things. He would be with his people.

I would be with my heart.

"Yeah, but I can't stay here. I would drown here, Eoin. Much like I was before I met you. I am the one who wants to go. You're not making me," I finally said. "Happiness never found me here. I feel at home in Scotland. You know, before I went inside the book that day it called to me, I had a dream. It was so realistic. I was running through a field of heather with a man whose face I couldn't see. He and I touched hands for a brief moment and then we were pulled apart. And I was so frantic because I had to find him. I woke up all sweaty and bothered.

"It took me so long to figure out who that man was and what the dream meant exactly. And also why the book called to me that day. The man was you, Eoin. And we were being pulled apart by time while we ran. You were pulled from me, and I was trying to find you, even when I didn't know you. But my soul did. And the book pulled me in because I was meant to be there with you; to save you and for you to save me. I was suffocating here without you, Eoin. But now that we're together," I took his hands. "I can finally breathe. And losing my best friend sucks royally, but I have no doubt that she will do just fine without me. She's bubbly and outgoing and she will find a new roommate in no time. Probably someone who prefers dresses. And we will stay in touch. That's what friends do."

"And I can visit anytime I want, right?" Jessa said, startling me.

"Of course."

She came closer and handed Eoin a book which he took and looked over. "What's this?"

"It's the most important book you'll ever own, Eoin. It's the guide for protectors, so guard it with your life you crazy Scot! And if you lose it, I'll come to Scotland and rip out all that blond hair."

He held it close and promised to never lose it. Eoin went back into the room to pack it in his bag.

"I promise to take care of Fred," Jessa said, which reminded me I was also giving up my crazy cat. They needed one another more than ever. While I had been gone, they formed an unlikely bond, and I couldn't take that away.

"I finally signed up for that design school," Jessa told me. "I didn't tell you because I was waiting on their response."

"Well?" I asked.

"I got in! I'll be attending in the fall and my parents are so pissed," she laughed. "So I'll be moving anyway. Yep, me and Fred will be moving to New York City. She'll be a city cat before you know it."

I grabbed her and wrapped her in a hug. This was the best news I'd heard all week. Jessa was destined for design.

"Maybe I'll see your fashions on TV!" I said hopeful. "You have more talent in your pinkie finger than most people have in their whole body, Jessa. You will pave that city in gold when you're done!"

"More like glitter. Which reminds me," she said, "Let's take a look at which clothes you are packing for Scotland, shall we."

Oh man, I was in trouble.

****

Saying goodbye to Jessa tore my heart out and my eyes were still puffy when the Uber pulled up to my mother's house. I had to say goodbye to her before we left. Eoin and I got out and were instantly greeted by a different dog than Tuck. This dog was younger and lighter in color.

I bent down and patted him on the head. "Hey puppy," I said.

"That's Georgia," said my mom as she came out of the house. "Tuck died last month. I buried him out back if you want to go say goodbye to him."

She was expecting this visit. I had text her to let her know I was moving and that I would stop in and say goodbye before I left.

"That's all right," I said. "He's not really there anymore."

She shrugged. "Yeah, that's true. He's in doggy heaven. He was an old dog Savannah. You know that."

I did, but it didn't make it hurt any less. Mother looked good. She had color to her cheeks that I hadn't seen in ages.

"Have a seat," she said to me and Eoin, pointing to a nice little table on the front porch. "I'm Diane."

She held out her hand to Eoin and he took it and shook once. We were working on greeting people. It was a work in progress. The past month that he was here, I had taught him so much about living in the 21st century. It's been tough, but he was a fast learner.

"Eoin," he said. "I'm pleased to meet you finally. Thank you for allowing me the honor of loving your daughter."

She stood back and said, "Wow. Okay, you're welcome."

She laughed a bit and it was a nice sound to hear from her. I guess she was really working on her personality. I could already see a difference. It figures that now that I was moving she would change.

I sat down and she went inside and brought back out tea and cookies. Eoin sipped it and made a face. Her tea was always really sweet.

"So, Scotland," she said.

"Yeah. It's his homeland and I found a job there already. It's a small town library. I'd be the media specialist. It's a start. The school is nearby so I can finish my degree."

"And preserving?"

"Is still possible of course. I won't give that up." I could feel myself becoming defensive.

"Well, good. You're good at it, I'm sure. Just do what makes you happy Savannah. I really do want you happy," she said, her eyes on me. "I am sorry for how I treated you. You were right you know?"

"About what?"

"When you said that dad leaving changed me. It did. I resented him and you. I felt like I had no purpose and I didn't see that my purpose was raising you until it was too late. Savannah, don't make the same mistakes I did. Love those around you and be happy. If moving to Scotland is what makes you so, then good for you. But I ask one favor."

"Okay."

"Can we talk once a week? Can I have another chance at being your mom?"

I nodded and set down my tea. "I thought you'd never ask."

When we hugged I felt like I was hugging my mom and not the cold woman that she was the past several years. I had already lost my dad, so losing her had killed a part of me. Even as tough as I had acted when it happened, it did kill me. I liked to hide my feelings, but I decided, since meeting and falling for Eoin, that I wouldn't do that anymore. There was no need to hide any longer.

Twenty-Five

Eoin and I left my mother's and headed for the airport. As much as I hated to fly, I had to be strong for Eoin. He had never even seen an airplane before. As we drove closer to it, Eoin grabbed my hand and yanked, getting my attention.

"That? We're going on that?" He pointed to a large plane landing on the tarmac. I nodded and took his fingers in mine.

"We've been over this and over this. You will be fine, Eoin. We can have some beer once we're up in the air if you like, to calm your nerves."

He looked at me and nodded. "But we aren't of age yet. Are we in this time?" The last part he whispered. He was getting used to laws and rules and always said, "There are too many rules to follow." While I agreed, I knew there were reasons for them.

"In Scotland the drinking age is 18, so we're okay."

"Ah, good, 'cause I need a drink. Ye know, to calm my nerves."

We both laughed, hiding our nerves and our driver

pulled up in front of the airport. We got out and got our bags from the back. Placing mine on the sidewalk, I told him, "Stick with me, Eoin and this should go smoothly." Whenever we entered busy places Eoin tended to get lost or confused. This was air travel with a man from a time long ago. I bought illegal IDs for him and I wasn't sure what was going to happen. The man who sold them to me assured me that it would be fine, but he wasn't the one about to show them to the ticket agent. Nerves raged through me, but I remained calm on the outside.

"Hello," she said. "Do you have your boarding pass and IDs?"

We both handed them to her, in unison and smiled. I began praying she didn't find anything odd. Eoin gripped my hand and I did the same. I knew we were both anxious and would be fine once we got passed security.

"Okay, everything looks good. Enjoy your trip!" Thanking her, I took the tickets and IDs before she changed her mind. Security was next. No matter where I traveled I always got nervous going through security. Perhaps it was the roughness of the way they talked to me or handled my bags, but they were never nice.

"Oh this part," Eoin said, biting his lip.

"Just do as I do and you'll be all right."

I walked up and put my carry on onto the belt and removed my shoes. Eoin copied my moves and walked barefoot behind me. He looked at me and didn't look away. His nervousness was apparent, and that was never good in this situation.

"You to the left," the guard told Eoin, staring at his kilt and shaking his head. I swallowed nervously as Eoin went to the left of the line. He had to be wearing his kilt today, of all days. I couldn't tell him what to wear and what not to wear, but the security guard looked at him strangely.

"What's under that?" he asked, pointing to his kilt.

Eoin smiled. "I get asked that a lot. But if ye like, I can show ye?"

The guard didn't laugh instead he said, "That's okay. You can come this way with me."

"Ma'am!" I looked up to see an impatient female guard waiting for me to walk through the metal detector. I did what she said and hoped Eoin was behaving himself. He tended to make jokes that people didn't get. One, because they weren't Scottish and two because they weren't from the middle ages.

I grabbed my stuff from off the belt and put my shoes on quickly. I found Eoin talking with the security guard, as he patted him down. He was telling him about Scotland and how bonnie it was. The guy didn't care, but Eoin kept talking on and on. Finally, the guard made Eoin walk through the body scanner. Freaked out didn't describe the horror on his face as he put his hands up and the machine whirled around him.

"Okay, you can go," the guard told him. "And a word to the wise, don't wear a kilt to the airport if you don't wish to be questioned, 'kay?"

Eoin nodded and took his things. We had made it and were ready to embark on our final destination together.

As we boarded the plane I couldn't help but wonder what life in Scotland would be like with him. We had spent every waking moment learning about one another, and I wondered if it was enough to keep him loving me. As we sat down I asked him the question that had been bugging me all day.

"What if you regret your decision? What happens?"

His eyes went big and his excited smile faltered.

"Regret you? How could that be?"

"No, I'm serious. Living together, alone, in a foreign country could put a strain on any relationship. With us, it's still fresh and new. And I'm worried that it will hurt us, moving in together and well... it's a big step."

He took my hand in his. "Do ye not want to move with me? If not, well we can go back to your home for a while. I can get a job and we can spend more time there."

I shook my head. That wasn't what I wanted, at all. I had already told him that. But just the fact that he was so willing to do what I wanted made me feel secure. I should have felt fine about this.

"I want to be in Scotland, with you. I do. I am just worried. I'm scared Eoin. I don't want to lose you."

Bending his head closer to mine he said, "I understand now. You're afraid of the very thing that keeps me up at night. I watch you as you sleep and wonder if the book will suck me back in if I close my eyes. I worry that you'll tire of me. But nothing, at all, could drive me back. I chose you Savannah. You and your time. I don't want to go home, because my home is where you live and whatever time you reside."

Epilogue

I watched from the bed as Eoin dressed for the day. He put his shirt on first, then his kilt, and finally the tartan across his chest. It was a sight that I'd never tire of. His smile was broad and bright. He was happy. I was happy. Living in Scotland for the past year had been amazing. Granted it was an adjustment on both our parts. Shocking, too. Eoin had seen the major difference that had taken over what he thought Scotland was. His home was gone and in its place was a Scotland that I could fit in, but he had to learn to love. The hills, moors, and beauty of his home hadn't changed, but we had to travel to see those parts. We settled in a small town that was calm enough for Eoin to adjust, and also had enough that would keep me used to what I had known in life. Like a big library, a school, and a few quiet pubs. My dream of working in an archive had to be put on hold until I found the right schooling for it. But until then I enjoyed my job in the local library. I was near books, like I wanted to be, and still able to finish school. The college was nice and so were the students. Making friends with my classmates allowed me to see so many things about

Scotland, and this town.

It had taken me twenty years to actually be able to say that I was indeed happy; all my life. My birthday had been spent here in Scotland and with Eoin beside me. But there wasn't a day that went by where I regretted my decision. I had left it up to Eoin, and he helped me make my choice as well.

"Must you go?" I asked as he grabbed his things. "Don't you want to snuggle up in bed with me by the fireplace?"

Pulling aside the blanket I revealed myself to him, to entice him to come back to bed and fall asleep with me.

He came over to me and sat on the edge of the bed. "Lass, all I want to do is stay here in this bed with ya. But I cannot. I must go and you know that. It's a serious matter and they're counting on me."

I rolled my eyes jokingly. "Oh sure it is. But laying here with me in bed is a serious matter as well!"

He growled and pulled me into his arms, lifting me from the bed. "You're making this hard for me, Savannah. I cannot resist your beauty, but the men, they count on me."

He placed me back on the bed and covered me up. "I'll see you there?"

I nodded and planted my face into my pillow. "After my nap."

"Nap? It's ten o'clock woman."

I grumbled and he left. I hated when he did that. Tired was not the correct word for what I was. Staying up late to study for finals and traveling after was making me exhausted. Jessa said that I was doing too much. She was right. I shouldn't be preserving during finals but I was getting so close to finding answers on my latest historical study.

I traveled last night, after a full night of studying,

and got all that I needed. Eoin pulled me back in time and we celebrated with a bottle of champagne and chocolates as I readied the book for sealing. It would be sent to the Historical Society of Libraries tomorrow. Getting up, I pulled on my robe and watched as Eoin got into his car. He had learned so much so fast. It was crazy that he had only been here for a year. It wasn't always this easy. Some days were a struggle. He would mourn the friends and family he lost; especially around the holidays. For Christmas, we flew home and spent it with Jessa, who also flew in, and my mother. It made it easier when Eoin had people around him; which explained why he stayed at Malcolm's castle so long after telling Ainsley he had died. He didn't like being alone.

So when we got home from that trip, I made it my mission to get him a job. We found a tour guide position that was perfect for him. He spent the days going over the history of a time he lived through to visitors from all over. Living that history made him the perfect tour guide. And some days, like today, he was part of the town's historical celebration. He was playing the part of the Scottish Highlander for a reenactment ceremony. People from all over would attend and that made him nervous, so I did my best to support him.

I dressed in a new plaid dress that Eoin thought would match his father's tartan, which he wore today. Little did anyone know, Eoin's costume was not costume at all? It was all authentic and only Eoin and I knew that information.

I still hated dresses, but for Eoin, I would wear anything; funny how we change for our significant other. After curling my hair and throwing on a little lipstick, I was out the door.

Our town was quaint and small enough that walking

down the cobblestone paths to the park where the ceremony was being held, was easy for me. Besides, it wasn't raining today; yet. Scotland rained so much that everywhere I went I brought an umbrella. Getting used to the wet weather wasn't hard, just another adjustment.

I could hear the cheering of the crowd as I crossed the bridge over the river. The people of our town got excited when festivals occurred and I could see why. They were proud of their heritage and history. Today though was different. They were celebrating a man who had saved many lives in the 14th century, Sir Malcolm Walsh. And though I had only met him a few times, posing as a servant, I thought he was a genuine man who would do anything for his people. Unfortunately, due to the tumultuous times he was thrown into hiding, and he wasn't the best father to Eoin. But even Eoin would say his father was brave for leading the armies against the British. They fought many battles that prevented more death from spreading across Scotland.

I could see Eoin now as I entered into the fray. The crowd roared as he rode in on his black stallion. He held up the Scottish flag, portraying none other than his father. When they asked him to take the role, he battled with the decision.

"I am not sure I can be him in front of all of those people," he had said.

"Eoin," I told him. "There is no one who could bring honor to your father's memory better than you. Can you imagine anyone else doing the role?"

With that he shook his head and his mind was made up. Seeing him now as he rode bareback on this beautiful horse, gave me chills.

He rode around screaming, "For Scotland, we fight!

For Scotland we are brave!"

In that moment I saw his father for the first time. There were many times I had searched for Sir Malcolm in his face, but when he was yelling and screaming for his country, I saw it. We all cheered and it felt for a moment like we were back in the middle ages with the real Malcolm.

"Aye, he's got the blood all right," a lady said next to me. "You can tell he's a Walsh. I bet he brings his ancestors great honor."

I nodded as tears of pride welled in my eyes. I had changed Eoin's fate by bringing him here, but I didn't change a thing for Sir Malcolm. The English never saw how Malcolm had actually died but they reported that they had killed him with the help of a Scottish man by the name of Finn. Finn was an outcast and hated all throughout Scotland, harsh yes, but he shouldn't have stolen from me, and he did go against Sir Malcolm by doing so.

There were rumors that they lied and that Malcolm lived peacefully avoiding English patrol altogether. I wished that were how it really did play out. I wondered if Ainsley ever told anyone the truth, but with the rumors that were spread this far into history I could only guess at yes.

Seeing Eoin ride on that horse, I didn't care what history reported. We didn't hurt history even though we did change it.

After he went on to finish his speech and his ride across the park, Eoin came up to me on the horse.

"What a beautiful lass ye are. Fancy a ride?" He held out his arm and I took it as he pulled me in front of him. I shrieked not expecting him to so easily place me on the stallion.

"Wow, you are strong," I teased. "What did you say your name was?"

He laughed and nestled his nose into my hair, "My name is Eoin Walsh, but you can call me yours. What's yer name, lass?"

"You can call me whatever you want."

"How about *bhean*?" I looked down as Eoin presented me with a freshly picked thistle. Tied to it a ribbon. I took the flower, not remembering what *bhean* meant. I played with the ribbon and as it hit the sun, it shined brightly. It wasn't alone, it held a diamond ring.

"Eoin, what?"

"Wife. *Bhean* means wife. Will you?"

Shocked and completely surprised, I said, "What?"

I knew full well what he was asking me but I couldn't think straight. Was this really happening to me, to us? Were we ready for such a step in our relationship?

"Lass, I love you. This ye know. I know we are but young, but there is no one but you. I want you forever and I know you want me forever, too. Do me the honor and marry me?"

I turned around, hating that I couldn't see his face. For a moment I paused, trying to imagine a life without Eoin in it. We had been through so much together and we came out of it alive and in love. We had one another, moved across time, and across the world together.

I nodded and kissed him as hard as I could. When I pulled away my lips were swollen and tingly.

"Is that a yes?"

"Yes, it's a yes. Of course I'll marry you." We were ready for this step.

We rode up the hill to overlook the town that was now our home. I was happy and still shocked when Eoin got off his horse and pulled me into his arms.

I wrapped my arms around his neck and he worked

the ring free from the ribbon.

"Here," he said, pulling my left hand free. He placed the ring on and it fit snugly. "We are now one."

"Well, not until the wedding, officially. Besides, don't you feel like we've been one since the day you gave me that first thistle? Like that peace offering was the thing that bonded us?"

He nodded. "Yes. I suppose that's true. I never looked at it like that. But that flower was what brought us together."

"And a flower is what sealed our fate. Forever."

Eoin looked at his watch and cursed lightly. "Lass, you're going to be late for work. And we must get that book sent off, do we not?"

He was right. I had my shift at the library. With Eoin as my guide now, I was always on time for work, and traveling. And I was always safe. I enjoyed my job, but nothing was coming between this moment.

"I think I can call off work and we can celebrate tonight instead. Besides, I would much rather be with you instead of all those amazing tomes. There is something so much hotter about a Scotsman who proposes to you. We are going to enjoy celebrating this momentous occasion."

He nodded. "Aye, I agree. But you're giving up your books for me then, are you?"

I laughed. "I didn't say that. Don't go crazy. Just for tonight. We have plans for a wedding to discuss and phone calls, too. Jessa is going to scream so loud."

I laughed and Eoin nodded. "I'll stay clear of the phone when ye tell her the news."

The first drop of rain hit my nose and Eoin searched for something to cover me. I had left my umbrella on the ground when he rode up to me. Oh well. The rain came and it poured on us there on that hill. As it drenched us we were safe in one another's arms. This country could throw whatever it wanted at us, nothing would dampen our news or tear us apart. Not even the duty that I had to live up to as a Librarian.

I was thankful for my gift for different reasons now. I used to love the fact that it allowed me to travel through the most incredible times in history, and still did, but I was thankful to Harold Lockhart for writing the formula for a much different reason now. Even though I broke all the rules, I was thankful because without my gift, I wouldn't have Eoin. And I wouldn't have found my true self. That might be the most important thing. Getting lost in time was the best thing that ever happened to me. Sometimes you need to become lost in order to be found.

The End

Acknowledgments

First and foremost to my husband, thank you for allowing me to write my fourteenth book without one single complaint. Girls, thank you for going to bed on time so mom could write. Love you to the moon and back.

To my family at CHBB, I adore you all.

Royals, I thank you for yet another year of support.

Lastly to my readers for spending their money on my books and for taking the time to review them.

About the author

Christy Sloat resides in New Jersey with her husband, two daughters and her Chihuahua, Sophie. Christy has embraced the love of reading and writing since her youth and was inspired by her grandmother's loving support. She loves adventurous journeys with her friends and can be known to get lost inside a bookstore. She is the bestselling and award winning author of fourteen novels including, The Librarian, The Visitors Series, The Past Lives Series, and the Slumber Duology.

Made in the USA
Monee, IL
03 June 2021

70100283R00111